DEATH MAKER

BOOKS BY J. C. MCKENZIE

The Lark Morgan Series

Death Stealer (*prequel*)

Death Maker

Death Raiser (*forthcoming*)

Death Taker (*forthcoming*)

Isle and Eyrie Series

Cormorant Run

Heir of the Eyrie

House of Moon and Stars

The Night House

House of Chaos

Crawford Investigations

Conspiracy of Ravens

Nevermore

Queen of Corvids

The Call of Corvids

From the Shadows

Into the Fire

Dark Legacy

Embrace the Flame

The Carus Series

Shift Happens

Beast Coast

Carpe Demon

Shift Work

Beast of All

Obsidian Flame

Dangerous Dreams

Dangerous Liaisons

Dangerous Decisions

That Old Black Magic

The Good Griffin

Standalones

Immortal Throne (with Harper A. Brooks)

Call of the Deep (The Shucker's Booktique)

Stormbound (Be My Love)

DEATH MAKER

J. C. McKenzie

COPYRIGHT INFORMATION

Death Maker

Contact Information: jcmckenzie@jcmckenzie.ca

Cover Art: Tricia Beninato

Character Art: Kalynne_Art

Publishing History:

First JCM Publications Edition, 2022

ISBN: 978-1-990143-24-3 (print)

ISBN: 978-1-990143-25-0 (ebook)

To all the readers who love a dark tale and a slow burn

You're entering the creative domain of a Canadian author. There will be a combination of British and American spellings, a combination of measurement systems, and maybe even a little French thrown in to spice things up. You've been warned...

This book contains explicit language, ghosts, spirits, souls, skeletons, bones, violence, blood magic, necromancy and animal sacrifices (off-the-page as much as possible).

Please read with care.

"The power of death doesn't come from the loss of life, but from its impact on the living."

~ The Book of Life

Lark Morgan's
Rules to Necromancy

1. Never use your own blood

2. Never meet the Lord of the Veil

3. Never run into a barghest

4. Never reveal your lineage

5. Never take more than you need

CHAPTER
ONE

Blood sprayed my face, the warm thick liquid dripping down my cheek. The rest of the blood splattered on my black boots and the thick manicured lawn, but somehow missed the leather pants and vest I wore specifically for this job. I grimaced but finished the incantation to bring forth the spirit. My death magic pooled around me, dark and sticky, before driving into the bones laid bare before me.

The surrounding trees groaned, and an eerie warm wind swept over the gentle knoll in the cemetery. The loud hum of crickets and katydids filled the air, the constant soundtrack for a late summer evening. But another sound rose from the inky darkness of night.

A wailing spirit.

Ripped from the veil by my magic and pushed through the crumbling bones, the spirit of Agatha

Montgomery crystallized in front of me as a pale blue spectre of what she used to be, while the chicken's blood dripping down my hands cooled.

The sun had set less than an hour ago, and though raisings were common knowledge nowadays, necromancers like me still preferred to raise the dead at night because the barrier between the living and the dead thinned and it helped us avoid unnecessary spectators and judgement.

Pushing harder with my magic, I sent the spirit into the remains of her body. The corpse shuddered. Bones cracked and the wooden coffin groaned. Agatha's corpse awkwardly scrambled to its feet. Reanimation took bones, blood, and power, and I had all three.

Someone gasped behind me.

Dressed in her Sunday best—a tasteful, knee-length, dusty rose coloured dress with long sleeves, stockings with matching hat and shoes—the reanimated corpse of Agatha Montgomery waited for her orders.

Technically, I didn't need a reanimated corpse to speak with the spirit, but the drabs standing behind me did.

"Ms. Morgan?" The client's shaky voice spoke behind me. "Is everything okay?"

"Ask your questions," I whispered to the three people waiting. Placing the sacrifice in a sealable bag for the butcher, I set the package at my feet with the other three. If I didn't have to reanimate the corpse for the clients, I wouldn't have had to use so many chickens. I took out a moist towelette and wiped the blood from my hands and face.

"I won't be able to hold her long," I told them. That last part was a lie. I could hold this spirit for a long time, but I wouldn't. Spirits deserved to rest, not be dredged up by ungrateful nieces and nephews who bickered and squabbled over the estate and couldn't reach an amicable interpretation of a will.

I shuddered, squeezing my eyes shut. Nothing could stop my own internal critic.

Sell out.

Hypocrite.

I stuffed the soiled tissue in my pocket. I might not agree with my clients' motives. I might dislike raising the dead for trivial matters. But neither of those things stopped me from doing my job. The new world had few opportunities available for necromancers, and at least I could stomach this one and afford to pay my bills.

And Mom's.

Henry Montgomery stumbled forward and cleared his throat. He hunched forward as if he spent most of his time at a desk on a computer, and his wrinkled dress pants and crinkled shirt did nothing to make me think otherwise. He had a shifty hazel gaze and his fair complexion looked like he needed a healthy dose of vitamin D. "Hi, Auntie."

The corpse whipped her head in his direction and hissed.

"Auntie." Amanda Montgomery straightened from the other side of the grave, standing opposite of her brother. She tucked her blonde hair behind her ears and narrowed her gaze. She looked like a feminine version of her brother, just with longer hair and tighter pants. "We're sorry for raising you. We'd like to clarify your will."

Agatha hissed at her niece, too.

The third person, a court appointed adjudicator, stood expressionless beside me. Peter Schmidt had a tall, lean frame that fit his off-the-rack suit well. His pale skin gleamed under the moonlight and his keen blue gaze scanned the area. This wasn't our first time working together, and the novelty of necromancy must've worn off, because he no longer flinched at the raisings.

Peter had suggested my services to clients in the past. This wasn't his first rodeo and unless human nature or the laws governing necromancers changed drastically, this wouldn't be his last one, either.

While the court usually upheld wills, people generally had four main reasons to legally dispute a will and actually have a shot at winning—how the will was signed and witnessed, the mental capacity of the testator at the time of signing, possibility of fraud, or if they suspected the testator of being unduly influenced at the time of signing.

I didn't need to know which of the four reasons this particular case fell under for the niece and nephew to contest the will.

Nor did I really care.

It wasn't my business and I got paid either way.

"What about my will?" Agatha hissed again, her voice thin and reedy. "My last wishes were clear."

"You left everything to the dog," Henry protested.

I bit my tongue. The dog? Brilliant. I might love this woman a little.

"Not true." Agatha folded her arms over her chest. A bone snapped and her shirt sleeve ripped. "I gave you Harold's stuff and Amanda got my tea set."

Amanda squeezed her eyes shut, hopefully seeing how this wasn't going to play well for either of them. If only they'd apologize for disturbing Agatha and back out now. There was still a possibility of redemption for their asshole ways.

"How is Sir Edington doing?" Agatha asked, her voice sounding less tinny.

"He's fine." Henry said. "We don't understand how you would give all that money to a twelve-year-old pug. How do you expect him to actually use it?"

The aunt's true intent slapped me across the face. I groaned. Apparently, Henry and Amanda didn't have two brain cells between them to connect the dots.

I leaned over and whispered to Peter, "Who's taking care of the dog?"

His lips twitched. "The youngest sibling, Charlotte."

"Obviously, she got the brains of the family."

"She offered to look after the dog before the will was read. That's the real reason these two are fighting it. The will said the dog would go to whomever wanted him or offered first. Charlotte had to confirm she'd take the dog before I could read the next part of Agatha's will."

"The money goes with Sir Edington," Agatha raised her voice. "Your sister was always my favourite, anyway."

Henry and Amanda flinched before stepping away from the open grave, heads hung low. They didn't say anything else. They didn't apologize to their aunt for the intrusion, nor did they have any kind words to share. I already thought poorly of them, but I didn't often get the full story, so I tried to refrain from judging —and I certainly never let my personal opinions impact my professionalism.

This, though?

Their blatant greed, disrespect and lack of compassion earned my disgust.

Agatha keened loudly, her decaying body swaying back and forth. "Put me back, Bone Witch. Let me rest."

Ignoring the slur, I nodded and sank my power into the bones. Whispering an incantation, I sent Agatha's spirit back to the veil that separated the living from the dead. Agatha sighed in relief and her blue spectre of a soul faded away, returning to the veil where all souls gathered and waited either for rebirth or to move to the beyond where even I couldn't reach them.

The corpse fell back into the coffin, lifeless again, and already dismissed by the living. The call of crickets and katydids rose and slowly smothered the stillness that had settled over the cemetery.

Not getting the results they so obviously wanted, Henry and Amanda started walking back to their cars, leaving Peter, me, and a bunch of dead chickens in the graveyard. Still no thank you or apologies for wasting our time. No acknowledgement of their shitty behaviour.

I pulled a large plastic bag from my rucksack and dropped the smaller sealed bags with the chickens into it.

"What do you do with the sacrifices?" Peter asked. He didn't normally hang around to chat.

"I have a standing arrangement with a butcher in town for the poultry chickens like these." I refused to let the chickens go to waste. Their sacrifice wouldn't be used just for trivial disagreements and money. They would feed the hungry for a reduced price. I still felt like shit. Just not super scummy shit. "And if I can't get poultry chickens, I find laying chickens that are dying of cancer."

Peter nodded and glanced at the open grave. The

cemetery workers would seal everything up after we left.

"Does it ever bother you?" he asked.

"It?"

"The frivolousness? The lack of..." He waved his hand at the grave. "Respect. Remorse. Empathy? I don't know."

"Of course, it does." It did every day. These two clients hadn't tried to use their limited time with Agatha to say goodbye. They just wanted to harass her soul for their own financial gain, and I'd helped them do it for a fee.

"Then why do you do it?" He turned his kind blue gaze to me.

"I suspect for the same reasons you do." A paycheque. In a world that had grown less kind, people like me, people like Peter, found ways to survive.

"I tried to talk them out of it, you know," Peter said. "The will was pretty clear, even if it was rather eccentric."

"And now they'll have to live with what they did. They let greed and anger cloud their better judgment." Maybe one day they'd even feel bad about it.

Peter nodded and glanced at the grave again.

"If it makes you feel any better, I don't think raising Agatha hurt her so much as annoyed her. I'm glad the laws about the probate period are clear. Most souls haven't moved beyond the veil during that time. They're easier to recall and less disturbed."

"That does make it a little easier to stomach. Thank you." Peter swallowed. "Have you raised beyond the probate period?"

Did he honestly expect me to admit to breaking the law?

"For something else court related. Not wills, obviously," he added quickly.

Maybe he saw the shock on my face. The courts could order a spirit resurrected for many reasons, not just will disputes, and they weren't restricted by the same probate period as estate wills. And of course, there were the other raisings I did.

"I have," I said, and the memories sent chills down my spine.

CHAPTER TWO

I sat in the office chair at Raisers—the necromancer-for-hire company I worked for— and let the hot coffee slide over my tongue. Despite the clock saying ten at night, my ten roughly translated to a regular daytime office worker's four o'clock.

Roughly.

My hours generally shifted all over the place and the caffeine couldn't get in my system fast enough. The warm delicious drink tasted like heaven. Still early in the evening, I'd returned to the office to write up my notes and officially mark tonight's job as complete so accounting could follow up with invoicing for the final payment.

Many people envied necromancers for our work hours, but they only saw us magically appearing in a cemetery to raise one spirit before disappearing into the night. They didn't realize the paperwork that went into the job, nor how it drained our energy and left us exhausted.

Denise, a fellow necromancer with big blond hair, bounced into the large leather chair on the opposite side of my desk. Nothing about Denise was subtle. Big hair, big boobs, bold fashion statements and a personality to match. She was a whirlwind when she walked into a space, and everyone got sucked into her vortex.

Including me.

"Why do you look so glum? You're pretty much done for the night." Denise slapped a stack of files on the desk between us. Her floral perfume with middle notes of sandalwood, almonds, and something spicy wove around me like a magical lasso. "Before you head out, I wanted to give you these. I have some quality work lined up for you."

I groaned and straightened in my chair. "The last time you said that I had a spurned widower trying to murder his deceased wife's corpse."

"Yeah, that sounded awkward."

"It was." A memory resurfaced of the old man stabbing the reanimated body of his wife while he sobbed uncontrollably. I mentally pushed the images away.

"Even for you," Denise added.

Wait, what? "I'm not awkward."

Denise shrugged and reached forward to tap the top orange file folder with her perfectly manicured red nail. "Did you want me to summarize the jobs or not?"

"Yes, please, ma'am." I raised my hand to my forehead and saluted.

Denise rolled her eyes and leaned back in the chair. "That stack of files contains one will dispute, one widow closure, and three estate queries."

I groaned louder this time. "When will people learn and write a will?"

"What's the point? Half the time the ungrateful heirs will still drag you back from the veil to argue about it anyway." Denise shrugged. "Keeps us in business at least."

"That's shockingly insightful."

"I scheduled one per night, so you're really spread out over this week." She pushed away from the desk and stood up. "Oh, and that hot cop called."

"What hot cop?"

"You know exactly who I'm talking about."

"I do not." Okay, I might have an inkling, but I'd rather roll over in one of the graves I worked near than ever admit it.

"The hot cop you always do consultations and raisings for. He kind of looks like a younger Keanu Reeves." She snapped her fingers in the air. "Officer what's his name?"

"Detective Kang?"

"Yeah, that's him."

"He needs a personality to be good looking." I snorted.

"Honey, no one needs a personality to be hot."

I shrugged. Denise and I would have to disagree on that. She might be a whirlwind, but I was a willow tree. I would bend in the strong winds, but I'd never break.

"Did he leave a message?" I asked.

"No."

"Did he want me to call him back?" If he was at a crime scene, the case would be time sensitive.

"He didn't say."

I took a deep breath, not allowing my exhaustion to take over to snap at Denise. "What *exactly* did he say?"

"Only to tell you he called." Denise tilted her head, her blonde hair bouncing, before she walked over to the door. "Which I did. You're welcome."

"Thanks. You're a gem." If Kang needed me, he would've said it was urgent. He'd done neither, which meant I probably had to testify in court or fill out a form for him. That happened often enough.

"Toodles." Denise finger-waved over her shoulder as she slipped from the room.

With a quick glance at my phone, I mentally promised to check in with Detective Kang tomorrow. I wanted to go home. Even though tonight's raising wasn't that different from any of the other estate disputes I'd gone to, it left me feeling icky. I didn't feel like following up the experience with hours of filling out police forms or dealing with Kang's not-so-subtle dislike for me.

Maybe I was just getting old and cynical. And tired. My bed called for me.

I TOOK another half an hour to complete the paperwork for the sanctioned raising and review my cases for the week. The laptop in front of me hummed. Though our office building had air-conditioning, I preferred fresh air at this time of night and had cracked open the window behind my desk. Even though my office didn't have a thermostat or a vent for the air-conditioning, Denise would've scolded me for wasting energy if she was around. I'd closed my office door to reduce squandering the building's collective air-conditioning just the same.

The ocean wind outside rustled the leaves, and a steady drone of traffic trickled in, but otherwise, the night was quiet. Victoria was a city that bustled during the day, but often had prolonged lulls in the evening—a sleepy city, and tonight was no exception. Not even close to midnight, and the sounds from the city outside had already faded.

After closing the window, I shut the laptop, threw my work keys in my purse and left the office. I stepped from the air-conditioned lobby into the muggy night. So close to the ocean, and a variety of restaurants, the air always seemed to carry a mixture of sea salt, grilled meat, and summer floral scents at this time of year.

The office doors swished closed behind me.

Lingering heat from the day rose from the pavement and kept me warm as I made my way around the building to where I'd parked. Mentally running through the recent cases I'd worked for the VicPD, I tried to recall which ones might require a follow up from Kang and failed.

I turned the corner and skidded to a stop. Three vampires waited for me in the parking lot. Three vampires, all wearing expensive suits. Maybe to someone else they'd appear as living, breathing humans. Not to me. Their stillness gave them away more than anything else. I'd seen vampires before, of course, but always in controlled, safe environments. Right here, right now, I had no backup. No weapons aside from the sheathe knife in my pocket. No advantage.

I cursed.

Ever since I had a murderer abduct me after a job for the VicPD went wrong, I'd taken self-defence classes and my brother taught me how to use weapons, but none of those years of training would help me tonight. Not if these vampires planned to attack. My skills didn't nullify their speed.

The only thing preventing me from losing my mind and having a full-blown panic attack was the knowledge that most bloodsuckers didn't attack unwilling people, and these vampires looked a little too bougie to slum it on this side of town at ten thirty at night just to maul a random necromancer.

Their suits matched in that expensive coordinated way society presented successful businessmen in books and movies. All tall with black hair, brown eyes, and olive-toned skin, they looked like they could be brothers—brothers who modelled on Italian runways or billionaire romance book covers.

The vampires' death energy pinged off me, teasing and tantalizing. Like the smell of freshly baked cinnamon buns, the magic called to me and drew me forward. I could reach out and try to pull the power to me.

And if they sensed my intentions, I'd be dead before I took my next breath.

"We mean you no harm," the man in the middle spoke. His dark brown eyes tracked me, as if logging every movement, every heartbeat and muscle twitch.

There was something familiar about his face, which was odd, because I didn't make a habit of hanging out with vampires. In fact, though my occupation involved death, cemeteries and long night hours, my world rarely intersected with the undead.

"Pretty sure that's what all serial killers tell their victims beforehand," I said.

The man smiled, his full lips widening to reveal shockingly white teeth and long fangs. They didn't retract like the ones fake vampires had in the movies predating the Awakening.

Vampires, and pretty much every other kind of supernatural being, came out of the supernatural closet forty years ago. Known collectively as glamies for our supposedly glamorous appearance or ability to glamour, we could no longer hide in the shadows. Not all of us could glamour, either, but even that skill couldn't save us from the Awakening.

Social media, extra security measures on government issued identification, and a high-profile actor noticeably surviving multiple gunshot wounds while filming live made living incognito more and more difficult. The outing caused such a chaotic mess, historians now referred to the time as the Awakening—when mere non-supernatural mortals, or drabs, woke up and realized they were, in fact, not alone.

Canadian society still scrambled to work out the kinks in legislation that the existence of vampires and other glamies represented. We might be known as a "polite" country, but sometimes "sorry" didn't cover shit. A lot of high-ranking vampires spoke out regularly against the injustice and double standards within our society.

The vampire's familiarity struck me.

I swore under my breath as I placed his handsome face. Gregor Fissore, the Master Vampire of Victoria. All vampires in the area answered to him and he ruled them with an iron fist.

And here he was, standing on the uneven pavement of my work's staff parking lot deigning to speak with me, a lowly bone witch who struggled to make ends meet and pay her mom's medical bills.

I froze.

Or was he here about my brother?

I had a strict "don't ask, don't tell" relationship with Logan and his work. And for the most part it worked. His job rarely impacted our personal lives, and he worked extra hard to keep it that way.

Had someone identified him? Was his cover blown? Did something happen to him? Or to his boyfriend?

Fury welled up inside me, banishing the fear and doubt, replacing it with white, hot rage. I might back away from personal confrontation, but if the boys were in danger, nothing could stop me from protecting them. Not even death.

I reached out with my magic and brushed the death energy clinging to the vampires' skin. If they threatened me, I'd try to pull their power to me.

Maybe I could make them fall to their knees and beg for their undead lives.

And maybe they'd gut me before I had the chance to issue any commands.

I continued to study the vampire in front of me. He didn't look like he was here to fight. Maybe I should hold off on the attempt at smiting until after I figured out what he wanted.

The media had Gregor's face plastered everywhere. Women flocked to his clubs with the hopes of catching his eye while he raked in the profits. Keeping my magic ready, I glanced at the other men who hadn't spoken or moved. Security? Buddies? Gregor didn't have any known blood relatives, so despite their similar features, they most likely weren't siblings.

"'That's what all serial killers tell their victims beforehand...'" Gregor repeated my comment, his tone light. He spoke as if saying the words again would help him understand what I'd meant. "Not many would dare to compare me to a serial killer."

"The tabloids say you're over four hundred years old and a ferocious warrior," I said.

He cocked his head as if considering my mental state.

Stand in line, buddy. I hadn't figured out my own brain yet, and I'd been trying for years. "Maybe this is offensive to assume, but I'm guessing you've killed more than one person."

He narrowed his eyes.

"I'll take that as a yes." I hefted my bag on my shoulders, drifting my hand down to the pocket that held my sheathed dagger. "So you meet the requirements of a serial killer. Really, I'm just stating facts." Why was I still talking? I raised the dead, I had no wish to join them prematurely.

Gregor blinked.

Silence stretched and his companions remained frozen.

Gregor laughed, a deep rumble from the core. "I heard you were...different. I'm glad to find the reports were accurate."

I swallowed and somehow remained upright. Reports? What reports? What did they mean by different? And what else did these reports say? And why did they exist in the first place?

I might be a part of the glamy community, but I didn't party with the big boys. I kept my head down and worked hard. And if Logan rubbed elbows with the elite, it was the last thing they did.

"What do you want?" I asked, still holding my magic in check, ready to lash out.

Maybe Denise was right. Maybe I was awkward.

Gregor stopped laughing, but his disarming smile returned. He reached into his jacket and pulled out a card from the inside pocket. "I'd like to offer you a job."

I glanced over my shoulder at the building. "You could've just called the office. We have a nighttime secretary."

"I'd prefer this one..." He paused, presumably looking for the right words. "I'd prefer this off the books."

"I only work on the books." That didn't sound quite right, but, hopefully, he got the point.

"You haven't heard what I'm offering," he said.

I shook my head. "No amount of money is worth losing my license and livelihood."

Gregor clicked his tongue. "I wasn't offering money."

I stared at him. Was he delusional? What else

could he possibly offer me that was worth risking my license?

He studied the card in his hand and stepped forward, closing the distance between us. I pulled more magic around me. Necromancy might be a little useless against a living mortal, but I was willing to test its impact on a vampire with death energy.

"I know why you work so hard," he said. "I also know you're running out of options. She doesn't have much time left."

I stiffened. "Are you threatening my family?"

"On the contrary. I'm offering a solution."

I held my breath. He couldn't possibly be offering what I thought he was offering.

He nodded slowly as if he read my mind.

Hell, maybe he did.

"I will cleanse the blood disease rampaging through your mother's veins." He held the card out.

I swallowed and reached forward to take the card from his fingers. "What do you want me to do in return?"

"Isn't it obvious?" Gregor asked. "You're a necromancer. A very good one. I want you to raise the dead for me."

CHAPTER

THREE

I shut the door to my apartment with my foot and
leaned against the steel door. Closing my eyes, I
dropped my head back and focused on breathing
in the familiar smells. The last tenants had been chain
smokers and no amount of deep cleaning would ever
get rid of the faint scent of cigarettes that clung to the
walls. Layered on top of that was my brother's
favourite cologne, Brandon's aftershave, cat fur,
popcorn, and something else kind of floral.

Home.

This smelled like home.

Maggie trotted down the hallway and brushed her
fluffy white body along my legs before meowing at me.

"Have the boys not fed you?"

She meowed again.

"I'll fix that right away." They'd probably both fed
her, but I was a sucker for those big cat eyes.

She turned from me, lifted her tail straight in the air and strutted back toward the living room as if the hallway was her runway and I was merely a fan.

Pretty accurate, actually.

Maggie had come into my life when her previous owner had been murdered. Bernie still sometimes visited to see her cat, not quite ready to move on. Others might be put out or angry, but I actually looked forward to Bernie's visits. She'd been the one to tip me off about Ricky's cheating and I found comfort knowing I had a ghost looking out for me.

When Bernie visited, my brother Logan would shake his head and leave the room. He might sense her to a certain extent, but he couldn't see her, so it just looked like I talked to the air, and apparently, I "creeped him out." Me. His own twin sister. I was the one who raised people from the graves instead of putting them in one.

Logan's boyfriend Brandon couldn't see or hear spirits either, but he'd stay and tease me about sharing custody of a cat with a dead person.

Whatever.

I liked Bernie and Maggie was worth sharing. And right now, I could use some therapeutic cuddles with my cat.

After Gregor dropped his bombshell offer on me, he'd left as quietly and unassuming as he'd arrived, while I remained standing in the empty staff parking lot clutching his card. My mind still reeled.

The master vampire had offered to heal Mom.

When Mom first received her diagnosis for sanguimort, a rare blood disorder, I'd researched all possible treatments and cures, even this one, but blood cleansing required a powerful and willing vampire. Gregor wasn't known for his benevolence and out-of-town vampires cost more than the medical treatments my brother and I kept saving for.

Would I take the deal?

Maybe.

Probably.

Yes. Absolutely, fucking yes.

"That you, Sparky?" Logan called out from the kitchen around the corner.

"Yeah." I pried my eyes open and pushed off the door.

Logan walked around the corner and froze. Dressed in a fitted long-sleeved cotton shirt rolled up to his elbows and dark denim jeans, my twin brother was a taller, masculine version of myself. He joked that I got all the magic in the womb, and I usually replied that he got all the height. We shared the same brown-black hair, blue eyes, and taste in men.

"You look like shit," Logan said.

"Babe! That's no way to talk to our girl." Brandon followed my brother from the kitchen and casually draped his arm over Logan's shoulders. Tall, rugged, and built like a linebacker, Brandon was a handsome man with eyes for only Logan.

He studied me, his full lips turning down. "I'll get you a drink."

I turned to my brother. "Can we keep him?"

Logan chuckled and shook his head. Brandon had unofficially lived with us for almost half a year now.

"Seriously, there's no reason for him to keep paying rent at that other place." I cringed. Rent in Victoria was many things, but cheap wasn't one of them.

"I've been saying that for months." Brandon pulled away from Logan and play punched him in the shoulder.

An awful thought slapped my brain. "Unless you want to move out together." I swallowed. It had been just me and Logan since Dad disappeared, and Mom got sick.

Logan jerked back. "You can't get rid of me that easily."

I released a breath. "Thank God."

Brandon winked at me and slipped away to go back to the kitchen.

"What happened?" Logan asked. He didn't often ask me about my day, especially not when I was working because he knew how much the job took out of me and how I hated discussing that part of my life. Reliving the shame always managed to crush a little more of my soul.

"Did someone hurt you?" he asked. His focus narrowed in on me with heightened precision as he slipped on a mask of indifference. His body stilled and for a brief moment, I got a glimpse of my brother in work mode.

I was the only one in my family with necromancer powers. At least the only one alive. Dad had left years ago, so he didn't count, Mom was barely a hedge witch —able to conduct basic spells with herbs and a grimoire —and Logan...well, my twin brother had a completely different skill set, one that we didn't often talk about.

Necromancers represented a spectrum of abilities to utilize death magic, the weakest only managing to see spirits where the strongest could walk the veil. Some sources even claimed powerful necromancers had the ability to pull life from the living, control the undead and give spirits the ability to harm drabs in the living realm.

I'd never tested my abilities to the fullest. To try those latter skills, I risked death or incarceration. Despite turning thirty-one this year, I was still learning my limitations and often by trial and error. Both my grandfathers and one grandmother had been necromancers, but they were long gone by the time I displayed any power and the one person who could've taught me everything he knew about death magic disappeared fifteen years ago.

"Do you remember how we looked into vampiric healing?" I asked Logan, trying to distract my brain from falling down the rabbit hole of parental abandonment.

Logan's eyes widened and he dropped his scary

professional mask, turning back into a softer version of himself. "We crossed the possibility off our list because we couldn't find a vampire strong enough, willing and within our budget."

"Gregor Fissore came to see me tonight."

Logan paled. "No shit."

I held up my hands in the universal sign of help-lessness.

"Why?" Logan narrowed his eyes. "What does he want?"

"An off-the-record raising."

Logan stilled, his body a ball of tension. "You can't do that."

"Yes, I can."

"You could lose your job."

"A job I only tolerate to save money for Mom. And the money side of things isn't exactly going well. We aren't saving as much as we hoped, and B.C. Health Care is nowhere close to approving the experimental treatment so it will be covered by the provincial medical plan. The longer we take, the less likely Mom will still be a good candidate for the procedure."

Logan closed his mouth. He knew as well as I did Mom didn't have much time left. She'd already passed the doctor-projected expiry date.

Brandon walked around the corner with a glass of white wine. He glanced at my brother as he held out the wine, a silent question on his face. Brandon loved me like a sister, but no one ever doubted his loyalties. I couldn't have asked for a better partner for my twin.

"Thank you." I plucked the glass from his hand and took a deep drink. Having worked in a restaurant for years before getting my necromancer licence, I knew all the tricks to wine tasting, but I didn't need to do any of that crap. The best way for me to taste-test any wine was to just drink it. Besides, my wine came out of a box, and I always got the same kind. I had no illusions about being fancy. I took a long sip and enjoyed the full taste that had a nice balance between sweet and dry.

"What were we talking about?" Brandon asked. He pushed his curly brown hair out of his face.

"How Lark is going to make a too stupid to live move," Logan snarled.

"Oh goody. Those are always fun to watch," Brandon said.

"You make it sound like I make those kinds of moves often," I said.

"You don't?" Brandon fluttered his thick eyelashes at me.

"You used to be my favourite."

Brandon shrugged. "If you're looking to make some irresponsible decisions you should come out with us tonight."

Oh no. No, no, no, no, no. Going out with the boys would end with a splitting headache at best and a hungover walk-of-shame from a man-child's basement bedroom in his mom's house at worst. "Think I'll pass."

"Oh, come on," Brandon whined. "You never come out with us anymore."

"That's because you don't look out for me." I jabbed Brandon in the chest.

He had the audacity to look offended. His hand drifted to where I'd poked him and rubbed the area as if I'd just dealt him a mortal blow.

"How can you say that?" Brandon asked. "You're always safe with us."

"Safe physically, sure. But you don't try to stop me from making bad decisions. You encourage it."

Brandon relaxed and dropped his hand. "Oh, well yeah. You need it, babe. You're wound too tight."

"You need to make a few more bad decisions, if you ask me. Just don't start dating them like you did with that last asshole," Logan said.

"Fuck Ricky," Brandon said.

Logan grunted in agreement, slung his arm over my shoulders and pulled me to kiss my cheek. "Get dressed, Sparky. You're coming out with us tonight."

ONE WINE and two wardrobe changes later and I teetered on three-inch heels out the door with the boys.

After insulting my limited choice in outfits, Logan and Brandon agreed I should wear my leather pants.

"But they're for work," I complained. I wore leather all day, every day, as a part of the unofficial necromancer uniform.

"Those pants are still hot as shit," Brandon replied.

So, there I was, arm and arm with my brother and his boyfriend, wearing leather pants and a matching bustier, hitting the club scene just after midnight. Despite the wardrobe changes, we were efficient at getting ready. It helped that I took little time to accessorize. I kept my golden pendant on and grabbed a smaller clutch purse. Something in the outfit must've worked because the bouncer at the club let us cut the line and walk straight in.

We paid the cover and passed the coat check. With dancing and booze to keep us warm, we hadn't brought jackets. The club opened to a large warehouse-style room with a long bar running the entire length of one wall. Under the colourful strobe lights, a DJ wearing dark sunglasses and a ball cap bopped his head and did magical DJ stuff with his equipment on an elevated stage at the far end of the room. Between us and the DJ lay a sea of partiers. People bumped and grinded with and on each other, swaying and dry humping.

Logan pressed his hand to the small of my back and leaned in. "I'll get the drinks."

"Come on." Brandon grabbed my hand and pulled me onto the dance floor.

The heavy beat pumped and rattled my chest and the strobe lights glinted off my gold pendant where it sat nestled in my cleavage. Dancing with my brother's boyfriend was like dancing with one of my girlfriends except his presence kept the other guys away. I'd been with Logan when he first met Brandon. We'd gone to the bookstore downtown and found this fine specimen of a man in the Science Fiction and Fantasy aisle. He caught both our attention, with his strong build and rugged good looks, but after two minutes of striking up a conversation, he only had eyes for my brother. I'd wandered away to the smut section and left the men to their flirtatious banter while I perused books with half-naked men on the covers.

Brandon had bought Logan a book and asked him out for coffee and my brother was a goner. Logan deserved a man like Brandon. He'd had enough crap flung his way during his lifetime and deserved some good karma. Brandon was strong, affectionate, and attentive. He kept Logan in the light, bringing out his playful side and providing him relief from the darkness that haunted him from within.

Loving Logan, albeit in completely different ways, gave us something in common and Brandon quickly became another key component to our lives, and instead of having one brother, I now had two.

I was well into my second drink when I took a break and let the boys have some space to dance with each other. I leaned on the wall and tried to catch my breath.

"Hey, babe," a rumbling voice crooned.

I popped my eyes open to find a large man standing in front of me. The entire width of his shoulders blocked my view of the dance floor and the gray shirt he wore stretched across his chest and looked ready to rip apart if he flexed. The guy had spent a lot of time working on his body in the gym, that much was clear.

"Hey," I said. I didn't normally go for the gym bro type, but maybe the boys were right and I should make some bad decisions tonight.

He leaned in, his jaw clenching. He had fair skin somewhere under the tan—or maybe it was spray tan—and bright blue eyes that caught the strobing club lights brilliantly. He placed both hands on the wall, caging me in with his muscles. I had nowhere to go.

Alarms immediately went off in my mind. I might be in the mood for poor decisions tonight, but not this poor of a decision.

"Let's dance," he growled.

Maybe other women found his growl and overt dominant posturing attractive. Hell, if I was into him, I probably would, too, but it just added to the sense of dread clawing up my back. It was too much, too soon, and I wasn't interested.

"No, thank you," I said, turning my head slightly away from his intense stare. "I'm taking a break."

"I wasn't asking, babe." He pushed off the wall and grabbed my wrist. His fingers dug into my skin painfully.

Did this actually work on women, or did he flat out not care?

Before I had a chance to do or say anything, the man's grip on my wrist was ripped away, and Logan slammed him into the wall beside me.

Logan wasn't nearly as big as the guy. He wasn't as muscle-bound, nor as tall. But he didn't need to be. Something fuelled Logan from the inside, providing him with an eerie power to create death. Sometimes, on rare occasions, Logan talked about work and how he shifted between almost two different personalities. The way he described how he felt when the darkness stirred within him made me believe he housed a separate entity somehow—kind of like demon possession or how shifters had their animals. When I'd ask Logan more about it, though, he always laughed it off.

Right now, Logan had definitely let his inner grim reaper out to play, and a flash of metal told me he'd drawn a weapon. Logan pressed a small dagger to the man's throat and applied enough pressure for blood to trickle over the blade. Despite my wrist throbbing with pain, I leaned in, trying to catch what my brother said to the guy.

Gym Bro paled at whatever words came out of Logan's mouth—too low for me to catch. Instead of putting up a fight, my would-be assailant nodded. Bobbing his head caught the edge of the dagger and he winced.

Logan stepped back, his blank expression sending chills over my body.

Without a word, the man bolted, disappearing into the crowded dance floor and leaving urine scented air in his wake.

Logan had already made the dagger disappear. He probably had thirty more strapped to various locations on his body.

"I could've handled that." I crossed my arms over my chest. With all the training from Logan over the last six years, I would've, too.

"Of course," Logan said. "But death magic would've just given him the ick. I find a knife to the throat much more effective."

I snorted and dropped my hands. "I'll remember that for next time."

"Are you okay?" Logan peered down at me, his gaze sweeping my body and settling on my wrist. The rosy colour in his cheeks—probably from the dancing—drained away and he pressed his lips together. His gaze drifted to where the man had disappeared.

If Gym Bro was smart, he'd leave the club right away. If Logan ran into him again, he might not survive the second encounter.

"I'm fine. It's just a bruised wrist." I placed both my hands on his shoulders. "You're the bestest brother ever. Now go dance with your boyfriend because he's making sad puppy dog eyes at us from the edge of the dance floor."

Logan laughed and his scary killer mask slipped away. "Ice that wrist tonight."

I was going to make a very rude comment about wrists and wrist injuries when my phone vibrated in my pocket.

Logan winked at me and spun around to find his boyfriend waiting. He grabbed Brandon's hand and pulled him back on the dance floor and I watched them for a few happy moments before I let the vibrating phone pull my attention away. Pinching the corner of the device between my forefinger and thumb, I pulled it free.

Crap.

I'd missed three calls and a text message—too busy dancing with Brandon and having a good time to catch the vibrations.

Frowning, I flicked past the lock screen. The text message and calls came from the same unknown number, but the text message made it clear who had tried to contact me—Detective Kang.

He made a point of never calling me on my cell phone—as if the idea of me getting his cell phone number horrified him. He either called the office or let his partner contact me. He wouldn't break his six-year habit for nothing.

Taking a deep breath, I walked to the exit and

called the detective back. The night air hit my face at the same time he picked up, almost as if his voice made the air slap me.

"About fucking time, Morgan," Kang answered.

I held the phone away from my face and looked at the screen. It didn't appear possessed. "Should I hang up so we can try that again, or will you behave?"

"Why didn't you return my call?"

"I just saw all the notifications." I wrapped my arm around my chest as a defence against the cooler night wind.

"Not those. I left a message with your work. Your boss assured me she'd see you before you left."

"She told me you called after I got in earlier tonight. The message never said to call you back so I assumed it wasn't an urgent matter. The courts were already closed, and paperwork is boring. I wanted to go home. I was going to call you tomorrow."

Detective Kang growled.

"Do you want to keep snarling at me like some kind of rabid dog or do you want to tell me what this is about?"

"I have an active crime scene. The coroner released it an hour ago and I'm holding it for you."

"For me?"

"Yes."

"Right now?"

"Yes."

"It's one in the morning."

"Crime never sleeps."

I sighed and glanced at the club doors. I'd have to send Logan and Brandon a text to let them know I'd left. "Give me the address."

CHAPTER

FOUR

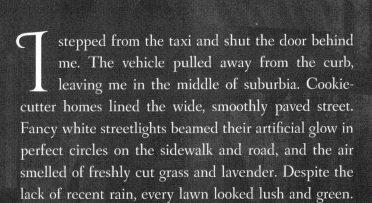

I stepped from the taxi and shut the door behind
me. The vehicle pulled away from the curb,
leaving me in the middle of suburbia. Cookie-
cutter homes lined the wide, smoothly paved street.
Fancy white streetlights beamed their artificial glow in
perfect circles on the sidewalk and road, and the air
smelled of freshly cut grass and lavender. Despite the
lack of recent rain, every lawn looked lush and green.
Residents here obviously ignored the water
restrictions.

One of the houses had yellow crime scene tape
cordoning off the yard from the others. This wasn't
the first time the VicPD had called me to a quiet
neighbourhood, and this reminded me of the first case
I ever worked with the detectives. Kang had called
me a bone witch and I thought I'd blown my opportu-
nity to impress the cops when the soul, Bernie,

wouldn't speak to me without us rescuing her cat, Maggie.

I found the cat and the killer and almost died for the effort. And Kang, of all people, had saved me.

Based on his subsequent interactions with me, he probably regretted it.

That didn't stop me from reminding myself every time we worked together that he had saved my life. If I didn't, I'd end up throttling the guy. Even with the mental reminders, I'd come close to committing a murder of my own a few times. The man was infuriating.

The cold air slithered over my exposed skin along with the feeling of death and something else. What the heck was that? I couldn't put my finger on it, but it had that annoying familiarity to it, like I should know, but didn't.

Yellow caution tape blocked off the area and a stoic officer stood guard with a clipboard, while others milled around the yard speaking in low voices.

Taking a deep breath, I approached the officer.

"Lark Morgan to see Detectives Kang and Jacobs."

The officer turned to me and held out the clipboard. We were about the same height, but she had a more slender build and unlike me, who Logan accused of weaponizing my resting bitch face, this officer wore a kind expression. She had dark brown hair and eyes, and a smooth olive complexion. I hadn't seen this officer before. Normally, I dealt with Officer Singh, but he'd transferred to Vancouver a month ago. This officer's name tag read Rodriguez. "About time. If Kang got any crankier we'd have to sedate him."

I took Rodriguez's offered pen, leaned over and signed in. "Do you think that would actually work?"

"Sedating him?"

"Yeah."

She frowned, seeming to think it over. "Even if it did, he'd still be a dick."

I snorted and ducked under the tape.

"I mean, he's a good dick," the officer added.

I laughed. "I bet he is."

The woman's cheeks flushed, a blush spreading across her face. "That's not what I meant."

"Is he inside?" I asked, changing the topic.

"They both are." Rodriguez pointed at the house in the middle of the taped off area and nodded. "Enter at the front. You'll need booties."

With a nod as a goodbye, I ambled along the smooth driveway, past the recently pruned lavender bushes. Though Kang rushed me to get over here, I never made a habit of running or jogging to a crime scene. Besides, these heels physically prevented me from any kind of serious cardio. I needed to find my centre—find my calm and relax my jittery nerves before I entered the chaos undoubtedly waiting for me inside.

Neighbours stood on their front steps, arms crossed over their chests as if giving themselves a comforting hug. They tracked my progress up the driveway. The woman next door to the crime scene, wearing a thick pink robe and bunny slippers, called out. "What happened? Is Addison okay?"

Seriously? What on earth made the attending necromancer more approachable than the officers, detectives or crime scene analysts? I wore head to toe leather and a perpetual frown. And given the number of techs milling around, I didn't need to see the actual crime scene to know things didn't look good for Addison.

I ignored the neighbour and took one step at a time to control my breathing. I'd been to a number of crime scenes over the years and though they were never the same, they all had something in common—death, grief and a depravity that I found difficult to put to words. Humans could be truly despicable.

Though the other detectives from Vic PD called me on occasion, Kang and Jacobs requested consultations regularly. And it wasn't because they liked me. I wasn't delusional enough to believe that.

They called me in because they were often assigned the messiest crimes, and I was the best at what I did.

I took another deep breath.

These detectives never called me for petty crimes or to chat casually over tea.

Nope.

Always murder and always gruesome.

I took one final long breath of clean air, nodded at the officer standing beside the door and stepped inside.

Artificially cool air flowed over me along with the smell of blood and the grimy feel of death. As a necromancer, I was exceptionally sensitive to the latter. Sticky and dark, death magic slithered over my skin, letting me know a death had occurred recently and the soul lingered in the veil. Just within reach. I extended my magic. So close.

Instead of drifting into the house to follow the call of the dead, I paused at the doorway to slip plastic booties over my heels.

Kind of ridiculous.

Normally, I'd change into the pair of running shoes I kept in the trunk of my car for situations like this, or I wore my boots with flat soles, but taking a taxi straight from the club meant teetering around a gruesome crime scene in three-inch, plastic covered heels.

I probably looked as silly as I felt.

A number of forensic specialists in full gear milled about the living room and dining room, collecting samples and placing them in labelled baggies. Their thick plastic coveralls swished with each movement.

Before I could enter the scene, the coroner had to release the body and the specialists had to process the scene, or at least the location where the body was located. While I raised the dead, they'd continue to process the surrounding area, working farther and farther outward.

I pulled my shoulders back and walked down the hall, my heels making a plastic clacking sound on the hardwood flooring. I slipped into the master bedroom at the end of the hall and took a moment to process what I'd walked into.

A brutal murder.

Blood spray decorated the headboard of the bed where a sheet covered the body on the blood-soaked mattress. Someone had stencilled "Live, Laugh, Love" on the wall above the headboard in flowing script, but now, the blood dripping down the wall made the words barely legible. Two men stood at the foot of the bed and quietly spoke to one another.

Detective Connor Kang stood to the right. I'd recognize his wide shoulders and arrogant posture anywhere. At least six and a half feet, he stood a few inches taller than his partner Detective Oliver Jacobs.

I swallowed and kept my focus away from the bloody scene.

"Did you bring a chicken?" I didn't bother to announce myself. The detectives always seemed to know when I arrived.

The men grumbled and turned around.

"About time, Morgan," Kang started. His gaze swept my body, and he jerked back. "What the fuck are you wearing?"

Jacobs whistled. "Looking good, Morgan."

I swivelled to face the blond detective and smiled. "Thank you, Detective Jacobs."

He smiled, flashing his straight teeth. He always looked a little sunburned, but now more than ever. With his broad shoulders, fit build and boy-next-door good looks, if he hadn't become a detective, he could've found a career modelling for real estate ads or starring as a quarterback in a Hallmark movie.

He wore snug fitting jeans and a thin sweater in the same cerulean blue of his eyes, and his blond hair was so pale it almost appeared white. When he wasn't burnt to a crisp like right now, his hair blended in with his equally pale complexion. He was good-looking, had a kind smile and a sharp mind, and always gave off serious golden retriever vibes.

"I heard you finally dropped that asshole," Jacobs said.

"Ricky?"

"Yeah, that's the one," Jacobs said. "Never liked him."

"When have you ever liked any of my boyfriends over the last six years?" I asked.

"That's a good point." He reached up to rub his chin. "You have terrible taste."

"Must be why I find you so attractive."

He winked at me.

Kang's gaze continued to travel down my body until he spotted my shoes. Something sparked in his gaze and his expression darkened. Obviously, he had a problem, and that problem was me. But he didn't say anything.

No, the asshole remained silent. He scowled, seemingly content to glare at me while I flirted with his partner. With Korean and Scottish ancestry on one side and giant asshole presumably on the other, Connor Kang was a specimen of a man to look at, but once he opened his mouth, he ruined his spectacular bone structure, flawless fair skin and full lips.

How Denise still considered him good-looking after speaking with him for more than five seconds continued to baffle me.

"You're overdressed," Kang finally spat out.

Okay, wow. He was still hung up on that. Besides the shoes, my outfit wasn't that different from my regular attire. Sure, the leather bustier was more revealing, but I actually had my work pants on.

"You pulled me away from my night off. I came straight here, as requested, instead of going home to change. And now you're making unsolicited comments about my attire."

Kang's lips twitched.

"You need to work on your manners, Kang," I said. "Shall I leave and come back in so you can practice those skills?"

"That won't be necessary." Kang leaned in and sniffed. "Have you been drinking?"

"Two drinks over about two hours," I said. "But don't worry. My buzz fled the second I heard your voice. Along with all the joy in my life."

Kang glowered at me.

45

Raising spirits under the influences didn't techni-cally break a law—at least not yet—but I couldn't be heavily inebriated for police raisings. My testimony would be challenged by any good defence lawyer in court.

Kang raised his eyebrows at Jacobs.

His partner shrugged. "She probably danced it all off."

"Do you have any other objections you'd like to make before we start?" I asked Kang.

"You wear an obscene amount of leather," he replied.

Jacobs choked, the colouring from his flushed cheeks draining away. He shifted his weight from foot to foot and his gaze darted to the exit.

"Easier to wipe off the blood," I deadpanned.

Kang grunted and turned back to the body lying in the pool of blood. Apparently, pleasantries were over.

"I like the leather," Jacobs leaned in and whis-pered. He always played the good cop to Kang's bad cop and I loved it. Anyone interacting with Kang for a hot second needed a little sunshine in their life and Jacobs was mine.

"Noted." I stepped closer to the bed and tried not to look too hard at the details.

"Addison Riley. Age thirty-five. Married. No chil-dren. Engineering consultant at a local firm." Kang read off his notes. "Brutally stabbed in the early hours. Neighbours reported screaming and called the police at three-thirty in the morning. First responders were on scene within seven minutes. No sign of the perpetrator."

Three-thirty a.m.? This must've happened almost twenty-four hours ago. It had taken a long time to process the scene and call me in.

Had the detectives even slept?

No wonder Kang had his panties in a knot.

"No sign of the husband," Kang added.

"He probably did it, then," I muttered.

Kang lifted an eyebrow. "Did the spirits tell you that?"

"You know I have to raise them first."

"And you know that's not quite true," he shot back.

He had me there. Free roaming sprits often loved to chat but that wasn't the case here. "I've heard you spout off enough stats to know you're already thinking the same thing about the husband. Didn't you say nine times out of ten it's the partner?"

"Honestly? I'm shocked you listen to me at all. You make a concerted effort to ignore me."

"I only ignore you when you're insulting me," I said.

He shoved his hands in his back pockets and rocked back on his heels with a hum. "I only do that every other crime scene."

Seriously? Ugh. I waved my hand at the bed. "If you already suspect the husband, why did you bother calling me in?"

I wasn't really complaining. Despite the depravity of crime scenes, I loved my work as a consultant. I felt useful. I felt like I was actually making a difference. I felt like my terrible death magic actually helped instead of superficially arbitrating wills for greedy beneficiaries.

"I missed you," Kang said, expression blank, tone flat.

I snorted.

"We had time to get a chicken. It's in the master bathroom," Jacobs piped up, interrupting my plans to throttle Kang.

I turned to Jacobs. "Hold this, please."

The detective frowned at the purse I held out.

Kang chuckled.

"I can't exactly put it down." And I knew Jacobs would actually hold my purse instead of chucking it into a pool of blood to spite me.

Jacobs snatched the purse from my outstretched hand.

As I turned to head to the washroom, Kang reached out and grabbed my arm.

I blinked up at him with surprise, but he wasn't looking at my face. Instead, he'd gently moved his grip and stared at the bruising skin on my wrist. He must've spotted the injury when I held out my purse.

"Who hurt you?" Kang asked.

"It's nothing."

Jacobs stepped in and peered down. He'd slung my

purse over his shoulder so he could lean in and run his hand over my wrist. "The skin isn't broken, but it's a newly forming bruise so it had to happen within the last few hours."

Kang nodded and finally shifted his gaze to meet mine. The ferocity I saw there sucked my breath away.

"Who did this to you?" he asked, his voice low and rumbling.

I snatched my hand away. "Just some jerk at a club. I handled it."

Actually, Logan had handled it but the less I waved my killer-for-hire brother in the face of the cops, the better.

Kang blinked and the murderous expression disappeared. He straightened and nodded. "If you say so."

I didn't have the time or patience to try to dissect what had just happened, so I headed for the private bathroom where the chicken waited for me instead.

Necromancy didn't require me to see or hold the remains of Addison's body if the death was fresh enough. Thankfully, I only needed to be in close proximity to her bones. The sacrifice and my magic would do the rest.

Sure enough someone had procured a live chicken and stashed the hen in the bathtub. With no cage, the animal had hopped out and pranced around the tiles. Poor thing.

I wasn't a vegetarian or a vegan, and I knew this animal would feed other people and provide sustenance, but it still sucked to take the life of an animal. I loved animals. I'd pet a crocodile if someone assured me it wouldn't bite my hand off.

Kneeling, I scooped up the hen, cradling her in the crook of my arm and ran my hands down her plumes and the soft brown feathers covering her neck.

"Do you have an evidence bag?" I asked as I walked out of the bathroom.

The two detectives had their heads bent toward each other while they quietly discussed something. When I spoke up, they quickly broke away, Kang with a glower, Jacobs with a smile.

The latter held up a sealable bag. "Right here."

"Clear the room," Kang said.

The forensics technicians glanced over at the detective. Almost in unison, they stopped what they were doing and left the room, clicking the door shut behind them.

Apparently, only I spoke back to Kang.

Interesting. That certainly explained some of his animosity.

I continued to stroke and soothe the chicken while I teetered on my ridiculous three-inch heels.

Kang was staring at the shoes again, judgement clear on his face.

Okay, I knew I looked ridiculous, but I'd never concede it to him. Especially not now.

I lifted my chin and pulled my shoulders back. "Do you have your questions ready?"

"Of course," Kang answered. "This isn't our first rodeo. Do you need a knife or do you have one hidden somewhere in all that leather?"

"A knife would be nice, thank you." I usually had a small dagger in the hidden sheath built into my work pants, but I'd left it at home.

Kang smirked and bent to pull a small dagger from his boot. When he straightened, he held it out for me.

"Thanks." I plucked the dagger from his hand. Cradling the hen in one arm, I took a deep breath and let my magic flow out and cover the bed. Death magic sought its own and found Addison's body immediately, smothering it like a preternatural seal, seeping past the flesh to find the bones. My magic sunk into the marrow and spread out.

I kissed the chicken's head, thanked it for its sacrifice, and quickly ended its life with the knife. Blood poured out and splattered on the floor. More magic flared to life and power surged within me. This close to death, Addison's spirit may still be around, which meant I wouldn't have to reach into the veil to try to wrench her spirit back to the living realm for a chat.

The blood around me hummed as the chicken's death fed the spell slipping from my lips. The air vibrated and a white spectre formed above the bed.

Kang gently took the dagger from me without being asked and moved off to the side to clean it and give me more room.

I had the power to reanimate corpses and solidify

spirits, but that took a larger sacrifice and given the cause of Addison's death, this seemed like a better option.

"Addison Riley."

The moment I spoke, Jacobs straightened and looked around the room. Drabs didn't have magic and most couldn't see spirits. This fact annoyed the crap out of both detectives, but especially Kang. His emotions showed in his tense mouth and the twitch in his right eye.

The spirit crystallized to show the mutilated body of Addison. Her head remained perfectly intact. Addison had been a beautiful woman with a heart-shaped face, full lips with a natural pout, and large, expressive eyes.

Her body was another story—one far darker and gruesome. Ripped open with a knife, flesh and guts spilled from her central body cavity. With the pale skin of her legs flayed, her muscles were left exposed, and they bunched oddly with each movement. The killer had focused most of the stab wounds around the chest, stomach and the top of her thighs—almost as if they had tried to amputate her legs after they killed her.

"Am I still pretty?" Addison asked. "Am I still beautiful?"

My stomach twisted and I swallowed down the rising stomach acid trying to bubble up my throat.

"Hello, Addison. My name is Lark. I'm a necromancer and I raised you on behalf of the VicPD. I know this is a confusing time, but we need to know who or what did this to you."

Addison blinked at me with her large expressive eyes before slowly looking down. Her hands patted her gnarled stomach and released a high-pitched wail.

I flinched.

Kang shuddered beside me. He might not see the spirit, but that didn't make him immune to the effects. His nose flared as if he smelled something bad and he curled his lips back, flashing those annoyingly perfect teeth.

"Addison, who did this to you?" I pressed.

Addison stopped wailing. Her wide gaze darted around the room until it settled on the bed where the physical remains of her mutilated body lay under a blood-soaked sheet.

The wailing started again.

I cringed.

Kang pinched the bridge of his nose. "Can't you do anything about that?"

"About what?" Jacobs looked around the room.

I narrowed my eyes. "I thought you couldn't hear them?"

"Just make it stop," Kang grumbled.

"I can't. I'd need another chicken for that and you only brought me one."

"Tight budget," Jacobs said, shrugging. "They've cut our funding again."

"And you don't come cheap," Kang said.

I sighed and turned back to the wailing spirit. "Addison, I'm sorry your life ended the way it did. Help us find the person responsible."

Normally, these cases went fairly smoothly. I'd raise the spirit of the deceased, they'd tell me whodunit, and boom—case closed. The police still processed the scene and found corroborating evidence for their due diligence and for their case if it went to trial. With a weaker, less experienced necromancer, the dead could lie, slipping half-truths and fallacies around the magic to seek revenge on someone else from beyond the grave.

Kang and Jacobs requested me because my power forced the dead to speak the truth. Not once had they finished reviewing the collected evidence and state- ments to discover a spirit had lied to me. Generally, cases were opened and after I got called in, they were shut.

I might be expensive, but I saved the VicPD tons on overtime.

But this? Not even my power could get a straight answer out of Addison. At least, not yet. Her wailing turned to incoherent sobs. The spirit sank down to sit beside her body.

Kang leaned forward, listening intently.

With a translucent hand, the spirit reached out to touch the blanket. Still mumbling, she stroked her head. "Darren did this," she finally said. "Darren."

Kang grunted and straightened.

"Does that name mean anything to you?" I asked.

"You can release her," he said in answer.

Ugh. He was always so stingy with details. He took his job seriously, and as a consultant, I didn't need to know the details of an active police investigation.

I pulled my magic and wrapped it around Addison's sobbing spirit while I also sunk more power into the bones of her body. Whispering the incantation, I sent Addison's spirit to the veil.

"Rest now, Addison."

Jacobs shivered and looked around the room again. Tension remained in his shoulders, making him hunch a little. "Is she gone?"

My limbs weighed a ton. Even my eyelids drooped. I didn't often do two raisings in the same night, and I especially didn't make a habit of hitting the club in between. With my power, I could do more, but that didn't mean it didn't come at a price. Sheer exhaustion slammed my body and I staggered.

Kang reached out, wrapping his hand around my arm to steady me. He stood unbearably close. Close enough that the subtle scent of his soft cologne wrapped around me. He always smelled good, and it was so annoying.

Leaning past me to look at his partner, he answered Jacobs. "Yeah, the spirit is gone."

"Did we get what we needed?" Jacobs asked.

"Darren," Kang answered.

"Ah..." Jacobs rocked back on his heels. "It's always the husband."

"Told you." I squeezed my eyes shut. I wished Jacob's comment and my initial instincts were wrong, but after working for six years as a police consultant, I knew this was one wish that wasn't going to be granted.

"Are you okay?" Kang asked. His dark gaze scanned my body.

"I'm fine." My other job often left me drained, which left little in the tank for experimenting with my power. I learned primarily from online forums and books, but testing out theories and rumours required energy, harassing spirits who'd earned their rest, and skirting the law.

I'd resigned myself to sticking with the status quo long ago. It paid the bills, and I didn't have the energy for more.

Kang nodded and let my arm go slowly. When I didn't keel over, he stepped away.

I found the evidence bag Jacobs had set aside and dropped the chicken into it. "I'll trade you."

Jacobs clutched my purse and looked ready to argue.

"Hand it over."

"I always get the chickens." He held my purse out and I plucked it from his hand and pushed the chicken bag into his chest.

"That's because you're the agreeable one," I said.

He smiled at that and held the chicken. "I'll make sure it gets to your butcher."

"We'll need your official report tomorrow," Kang said.

"Of course." When had I ever been tardy with sending over reports?

Kang stepped in again, placing his hand on the small of my back to steer me out of the room. "I'll call you a cab."

And with that, I was dismissed, and my night was officially over.

FIVE

The cab took off down the street as soon as I shut the rear door to the vehicle, and I sighed. I might be a fierce, independent woman, but was it too much to ask for the driver to wait until I was safely inside the building before he took off? The streetlights twinkled at me, and the still-ness of the street made my skin crawl—like something bad was just waiting to happen.

I clambered up the stairs to the main entrance of my apartment building and pulled out my keys. The boys were still clubbing, but I decided to head home instead of trying to meet up with them. In a well-prac-ticed move that I could accomplish with more than six drinks in my system, I shoved the large bronze key into the lock and turned. The mechanism made a loud click and I pulled open the large glass door. The familiar smells of home cooking, old carpet and perfume from the lobby flowed over me.

My phone vibrated in my purse as I stepped into the foyer of the building, my heels clacking on the smooth tiles. If I wasn't careful, I'd slip on the floor and end up on my ass. I'd done it before. Shoe designers really should put better grips on the bottoms of heels.

Dropping my keys in my purse, I pulled out the phone, and read the name on the screen.

"Denise?" I answered the phone. "Is everything okay?"

"Of course. I have a job for you," Denise said. Loud music thumped in the background.

"And it can't wait until the morning?" I asked. Someone said something in the background about having a job for Denise and a bunch of people erupted in laughter.

Denise ignored them and kept talking. "Technically, it *is* morning and it's a rush job. Triple your rate."

I sucked in a breath. "Why don't you do it?"

"I'm busy."

Ah, and Denise knew I rarely went out and assumed I'd be available. "So am I."

Okay, not exactly the truth, but I had a date with my bed and fully intended to keep it.

"Lark, please. No one else who can do multiple raisings in one night is available. It's triple your rate. You can have tomorrow night off."

"I have to come in and write a report," I muttered.

"What?"

"I just got back from a police consult," I said.

Denise swore.

That should've been the end of it. No one did more than two raisings in a twenty-four-hour period.

"I'll let the client know." She said goodbye and hung up.

I dragged my tired feet to the elevator and then down the hall toward my apartment and that hot date with my mattress. I'd reached the door when Denise called me back.

"Seriously, Denise?"

"He'll pay four times your rate," she said.

I opened my mouth to object, but Denise kept going. "You can sleep the rest of the week if you need to. Please, Lark." She dropped her voice. "I know you can do more."

"I don't have any chickens," I protested. I never did. What I meant was I had no way of procuring a sacrifice tonight. Most of the shops would be closed except the necromancy one but that shop was all the way across town.

"He has a sacrifice," Denise said. "I'll text you the details. It's one of the cemeteries in your neigh-bourhood."

I rested my head on the door. My brain hurt and my feet ached, but the idea of time off was so appealing right now. "I'll just change my shoes and head over."

"You're the best," Denise said before saying good-bye. Someone made another joke in the background. Honestly, they sounded like losers and Denise could do a lot better. But maybe she didn't want to right now. Maybe she was making some poor decisions of her own.

Lucky for Denise, she wasn't wrong about me. I was the best. I could do more. I could do a lot more raisings. It wasn't my magical energy that got drained during a job so much as my general mental capacity to deal with shit. This wasn't common knowledge, though, and I preferred to keep it that way.

AT THREE IN THE MORNING, instead of curled up in the comfort of my bed, I stepped from a cab and breathed in the fragrant night air surrounding the nearby cemetery. Now wearing sneakers with my leather ensemble, I looked even more ridiculous than when I'd teetered on three-inch heels. But at least I was comfortable and my feet no longer ached.

A man stood on the gentle slope of the cemetery lined with headstones. He wore fitted jeans and a bomber-style jacket with the collar flipped up to shield his face from the cool wind.

At least that was why I hoped he did it.

He also wore white sneakers and he'd tastefully styled his short brown hair with gel.

Normal. He looked normal.

And cute.

I shook my head and made my way up the path toward him. Some would wonder about my decision to meet a strange man in the middle of the night in a secluded area.

But I wasn't alone. The dead surrounded me.

Their bones called to the magic thrumming through my veins and attacking me in an area where I was at my strongest wasn't just stupid, it was fatal. I might not be capable of giving the dead power without blood or pulling spirits from the living—something that wasn't exactly easy nor legal to attempt or practice— but I could use the death energy to bolster my own strength and speed and thanks to my brother, use my dagger. I would be ineffective against glamies like the vampires who visited me earlier this evening, but this man reeked of mortality.

Plastering on my best customer service smile, I stopped a few feet from the open grave and the client willing to pay four times my regular fee.

"Mr. Harrison." I nodded. "My name is—"

"Lark Morgan." He smiled. He had great teeth and a deep, sexy voice. The moonlight made his fair skin glow. "Thank you for meeting me on short notice. Please call me Hudson."

I rocked back on my heels and nodded again. "As you wish."

He quickly raked me with his gaze, his attention snagging on my feet, currently snug in comfortable running shoes.

Everyone was a critic tonight, apparently. "It's been a long night."

"And I didn't give you a lot of notice." He waved at the gravestone he stood beside. "This is my mother's grave. Rose Lorraine Harrison. Your boss assured me you could reanimate her corpse so I could also hear her voice."

I nodded. "It will take more than a few chickens. I hope you brought them."

"Denise assured me a goat would suffice." He nodded to the left where he'd tied a black goat to a large tree.

My stomach sunk. Why'd it have to be a goat? I often dreamed of owning a hobby farm with fields of wildflowers and a horde of miniature goats to run around with me. Logan and Brandon had taken me to goat yoga for my birthday. And I often found myself on the goat side of social media because I watched all the cute goat videos that came across my feed. I loved goats.

I took a deep breath and collected my thoughts. "Yes, a goat will work. You are responsible for delivering it to a butcher."

He peered at me and hesitated.

"What?" Apparently, my customer service skills were tapped for the night.

"It's not every day you hear about a squeamish necromancer."

"I'm not squeamish."

"You just don't like killing animals."

I hated it, but the alternate wasn't an option.

"That's..." He flashed his teeth again. "That's endearing, actually."

Great. I'd finally achieved my life's purpose. My client thought my behaviour was cute. Maybe I could go home now.

"I will ensure the goat goes to the butcher Denise recommended. He will feed other families if the butcher feels he's acceptable for consumption," Hudson said. "If it makes it any easier for you, he's been diagnosed with an aggressive form of cancer and the owner planned to have him put down tomorrow."

"Thank you. That does make it easier." I peered down at the casket. The butcher might not take the goat if he had cancer, but at least I wasn't cutting the animal's life short. "I'm surprised someone dug up the grave for you at this hour."

"That's actually one of the reasons for the rush job. They had a cancellation, and I didn't want to wait months."

I nodded. The cemeteries loved raisings because they got to pull even more money from their clients, and by having limited availability, they ensured the demand kept the prices high.

"I'll open the casket if you bring the goat over," I said.

"Deal."

Hudson jogged over to the goat while I hopped down to the casket. Mahogany finish. Nice.

I snapped open the latches and pulled the lid open. The smell of death hit me first, and then I looked down. The decaying body of Rose Harrison stared into the night sky above. She wore a pink floral dress and a white cardigan, but death and time had stained the fabric.

Dirt tumbled down from above. Hudson had returned with the goat and now they both looked down at me in the grave.

"Can you give me a hand up, please?"

Hudson looked at the goat. The animal stopped trying to eat his jacket and looked over at him.

"Now?" he asked.

"If you want this done tonight, yeah."

He reached down and offered his hand. Standing on the edge of the casket, and using him as an anchor, I scrambled out of the grave and brushed off my pants. Usually, the undertaker used the hoists to lift the casket out of the grave for easier access, but it required machinery, time, and in these circumstances, more money.

The goat bleated at me.

"Sorry, buddy." I took the rope from Hudson's hand and knelt beside the goat. It trained its eyes with rectangular-shaped pupils at me and bleated again.

I reached out, scratched its nose and slit its throat. A kinder death than being shipped to a commercial slaughterhouse, but no matter how many times I told myself I was just doing the job of a butcher or vet, that this goat's life wouldn't be taken completely in vain, pain stabbed my chest.

Some necromancer.

Blood sprayed my leather vest and pants, and death swirled around me. The cemetery came to life. Bones screeched for release and spirits floated toward me from the trees. I harnessed the power and drove it down into Rose's bones, calling the spirit from the veil.

Nothing answered, but a tingle pulled at my senses. Rose was out there somewhere, but she was trying to evade my call.

I gritted my teeth and sunk more death magic into the open grave. "Rose Lorraine Harrison."

The presence of the spirit tingled in my mind. I reached out with my power to grab it, but it pulled away. This soul was a fighter. I dug deeper and deeper. Something broke. As if the seals protecting an untapped reservoir snapped, a well of power surged upward. I reached for the churning magic inside me and unleashed. "ROSE."

My voice carried across the cemetery, vibrating my

bones. My vision wavered, reality dropping away to reveal a hazy mist.

The veil.

I'd transported myself to the land between the living and the dead. Through the moonlit haze, a castle solidified in the distance. Skeletons on stakes surrounded the base of the fortress and luminescent spirits floated around the high walls and towers.

I blinked and the hazy imagery vanished, replaced by the quivering spirit of Rose Harrison. I was back in the living realm standing near Rose's soul as she floated above the grave with an angry expression.

"How dare you?" Rose spat. "Bone witch."

Instead of listening, I used the power from the sacrifice to send Rose's spirit into her corpse. Bones snapped and the wood of the coffin groaned as Rose scrambled to her feet and wailed.

Hudson flinched.

I sighed and sat down, my head spinning. My vision still wavered, and my magic, already waning, grew weak and left me exhausted. Either Rose was a spirit with super strength or I was more tapped than I thought.

"Rose." Hudson licked his lips and glanced at me. "I know you're angry."

"Angry?" Rose hissed. "Angry? You found a bone witch strong enough to raise me—I, who should not be pulled from the veil. You selfish coward. I'm more than angry."

"Think of Lily and Thomas," Hudson said, the crisp tone of his voice startling me.

Rose snapped her head back as if slapped. "Wh... what about Lily and Thomas?"

"Don't worry, they're fine. We all are. I'm taking care of them. But we need to know where you buried it."

"It?" Rose stilled. A gentle wind wove through the trees.

"You know what I'm talking about Rose."

Rose swayed in her grave and released a low keening sound that ran shivers up my spine.

"They need to be taken care of, Rose," Hudson continued, his tone softening. "Tell me the location and I'll make sure they're okay."

Of course, I could compel the spirit to spit out the information. At least I could on a good day. Tonight, I was exhausted. But even if I could, forcing a soul beyond sending them into their corpse crossed a line I preferred not to cross. Just because I could, didn't mean I should. I really hoped Hudson wouldn't think to ask. Angry customers were almost as bad as angry spirits.

"I want your word," she said.

"They will be looked after. Safe. I swear on my life."

Rose's empty gaze locked on Hudson's and she rambled off an address. "You'll find what you seek buried in the backyard."

Hudson nodded. "Thank you, Rose."

With the energy already draining from the spirit's body like water in a cracked bucket, I sent the remaining death magic from the sacrifice into the body to release Rose's spirit back to the veil.

The magic snapped away and I sank back, closing my eyes to find some calm. I didn't get long to rest. Dirt crunched and Hudson walked over to where I lay sprawled on the ground. I popped my eyes open to find him bent over me. He leaned down and offered his hand.

I slid mine in his smooth palm and let him pull me to my feet. I stood about a foot away from him and realized a few things.

He was taller than I first assumed, he had pretty blue eyes, and I was so done with tonight.

Instead of letting me go, he held my hand and smiled down at me. "Thank you for helping me."

"Of course." Though now I wondered how much money Rose buried and why Hudson was in such a hurry to find it. The amount of cash he'd dropped to get me here meant he already had some deep pockets.

"You know," he continued, still holding my hand. "This might sound a bit weird, but I'd like to get to know you better."

Say what?

He couldn't possibly mean...

His smile widened. He probably meant to come

across as reassuring and approachable, but I was too tired to appreciate anything other than my bed.

Was he asking me out on a date?

Sacrificial blood covered my leather top and pants for fuck's sake. This was a first. No one saw me slit a cute animal's throat, get splattered with blood, raise a dead relative, and go...hmmm...wifey material.

"Uh..."

"It's just...you're beautiful and not at all what I expected. I'm intrigued." He dropped my hand and ran his own through his hair. "It's kind of an odd moment to ask you out, isn't it?"

"I mean...your mom's body is resting in an open casket a few feet away."

He winced. "You have a point. I'm sorry."

I brushed off my pants again and dug my phone out to call a taxi. "Don't worry about it. I hope you find what you're looking for."

Hudson's smile widened and something flashed in his gaze. "I do, too."

CHAPTER
SIX

I didn't stride into the office at Raisers with confidence. I had no pep in my step or willingness to conquer the world with my go-getter trail-blazing attitude. Instead, I shuffled into the air-conditioned space as if I lugged around a hockey bag full of sweaty gear. The heat from outside clung to me and I paused in the entranceway to let the air chill my skin.

Denise walked into the lobby, a coffee mug in one hand and a file folder in the other. Her gaze landed on me and she changed directions, a wide smile spreading across her face. Today, she wore a white fitted tank top that showed off her breasts and flat stomach, paired with high-waist Capri pants that reminded me of the paper bag princess. When she walked, her whole chest bounced, and I often found myself torn between questioning my sexuality and chiding myself that I was no better than a man.

"You look like shit," Denise said.

"One, your powers of observation continue to amaze me." I let the door swing shut behind me. "Two, thank you. And three, you look amazing, as always."

Denise smiled and waved her folder in the direction of my office. "Come on, Sunshine. Let's get you caffeinated so you can get that report done and get some sleep."

"I knew I loved you for a reason." I swung my studded black purse over my shoulder and followed Denise's sashaying ass to my office. I hadn't lied. Denise always looked good, her hair and makeup always expertly applied, her outfits on trend and perfectly fitted. And today was no exception.

Me on the other hand? Hot mess.

I wore shorts and a tank top one size too big that showed a little too much of my pink sports bra and read: *I run for cupcakes.*

Normally, I would dress more professionally for the office, but I didn't plan to stay long. I just needed to finish the report and collect on Denise's promise to sleep for a week.

And think about Gregor's offer.

But was there really anything to think about? I already knew I'd do it. I'd do anything for Mom.

Denise swung open my office door and stepped to

the side to let me go in first. Amusement danced in my friend's gaze.

What was her deal?

I stopped in the entranceway to my office. A giant bouquet of lush red roses and crisp white baby's breath sat on my desk in a beautiful green vase.

"They arrived first thing this morning." Denise held out a card.

"Did you read it?" I plucked the card from her hand.

"It wasn't sealed," Denise said.

Of course, she read it. I snorted and scanned the little rectangular piece of card stock: *Thank you for last night.*

No name.

I groaned. No wonder Denise looked ready to explode. "It's not what you think."

"You didn't rock some guy's world last night?"

"When would I have had time for that? Three jobs, remember? That's why I look like roadkill right now. No, I did not rock some guy's world. Not unless you count raising his dead mother." I slid the card in my back pocket.

Denise pouted. "Boo."

"He asked me out," I offered.

She instantly perked up.

"I said no."

Denise flung her hands up. The disappointment in her gaze was palpable.

"I was half-collapsed and couldn't see straight and I'd just raised his mom. It didn't exactly feel romantic."

Denise sighed and glanced at the roses.

"Maybe I was a little too hasty," I said.

"Not all men are like Ricky, Lark."

I stiffened. I still hated hearing that jerk's name, still hated the sense of betrayal, shame and anger that the mere thought of him inspired. "I know. But that doesn't mean I have to jump on the first guy who shows interest."

"We are going to have to agree to disagree on that," Denise huffed. "Best way to get over one man is to get under a new one."

"We are two entirely different people."

"Got that right." She winked at me and turned to leave.

"You promised me caffeine," I shouted after her.

I FINISHED my report and sent it to the precinct after attaching my electronic signature. Hopefully, Kang wouldn't find any faults with it, and I could rest for the next century. Finishing the large latté Denise had presented me with, I tossed the empty paper cup in the garbage and started chucking my things into my purse.

The office phone rang, and I glared at it. The stupid thing kept making sound.

With a groan, I lifted the receiver and pressed it to my ear. "Lark Morgan speaking."

"Ms. Morgan. My name is Estelle Beaumont. I'm Gregor's human servant." The woman's voice had a smooth, almost creamy sound that reminded me of that calm feeling I got at an upscale spa. I relaxed, the tension in my shoulders melting away.

"Hello, Estelle. How can I help you?"

"Monsieur Gregor requests your presence tonight at his Victoria estate. Sunset."

"His estate? That's not exactly a cemetery." I immediately wanted to smack my forehead. Seriously, that was my first objection to this summons? I must be even more tired than I thought.

"No, it's not," Estelle confirmed.

Awkward silence stretched over our conversation. At least it was awkward for me. While I'd pretty much decided to work for Gregor, I hadn't had a lot of time to over-analyze my decision, and here he was, summoning me like a servant. None of that was Estelle's fault, but I was mentally running through possible responses and which options I could take that didn't end up with me dead. I didn't want to burn any bridges, either, especially when I planned to cross this one.

"Monsieur Gregor vouches for your safety and also wishes for me to convey a message."

Oh goodie.

"He said that coming to meet him does not signify acceptance of his offer. You can leave at any time, and he'll ensure you arrive safely home."

Oh. That was....that was entirely reasonable and not heavy-handed at all.

"I'll be there."

CHAPTER
SEVEN

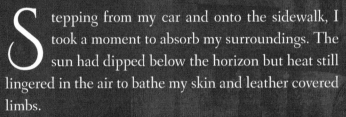

Stepping from my car and onto the sidewalk, I took a moment to absorb my surroundings. The sun had dipped below the horizon but heat still lingered in the air to bathe my skin and leather covered limbs.

Thankfully, after ending my call with Estelle, no one bothered me and I'd managed to escape the office, go home and sleep off my exhaustion. I woke up refreshed, and oddly more energized than usual. Just in time for my visit with Gregor.

I'd thought about the deal he offered. I looked at it from every angle possible, and I couldn't see any reason why I should refuse. Were there risks? Sure. Was the deal worth the risks? Absolutely.

I still needed to be careful and choose the right words and phrasing when I formalized the agreement with Gregor. I considered raisings appropriate payment for Mom's healing, but my indentured servitude for the remainder of my life, not so much.

The mansion I faced was so large it was almost comical. From my position at the front gates, I had to turn my head from side to side just to look at the building in its entirety. The most irritating thing about it was the house wasn't a monstrosity at all. It was beautiful. Elegant. West coast style, with a Cape Cod, wraparound veranda, a mature, well-maintained garden and the beautiful seascape on the other side.

Jealousy twisted my stomach.

Acquiring wealth might be easier to do if a person had several lifetimes to do it, but that didn't ease the pain of envy. I'd never own a house like this.

Estelle hadn't provided an address when she'd called. Nor did I need one. Everyone knew where the Master Vampire of Victoria lived and they either flocked to the area with hopes of glimpsing the popular vampire, or they stayed the fuck away.

I fell into the latter category.

Until tonight.

I stepped up to the guard in a black suit who stoically stood by while I drooled over his master's mansion.

"Lark Morgan to see Gregor Fissore," I said.

He dipped his chin and pressed his hand to his ear. He mumbled something too low for me to hear before stepping to the side. The gate swung open. The entrance must be controlled remotely because the guard beside me hadn't pressed anything other than his earpiece.

"You may enter," he said. "Do not venture off the path. Estelle is waiting for you at the main entrance."

I had no wish to meet my grave early, so I followed his directions and walked down the manicured cobbled path running alongside the driveway. My footsteps echoed along the stones. The buzz of nocturnal insects rose around me and the air smelled like the ocean as if I walked along a sandy path toward a beach instead of a thriving vampire den.

I paused at the front entrance, the sounds and smells of late summer and the thoughts of how misplaced they felt slipped away. With twin mermaids carved into the deep, mahogany wood, the double door entrance to the house gave me another thing to add to my list of wants. Of things I'd never have.

To an observer, I might sound bitter, jaded or envious, and while the latter might be true to a certain extent, the first two most definitely weren't. Money and riches weren't at the top of my list. Of course, they'd be nice to have, but they weren't in my dreams at night.

My family—whole, healthy, and happy. That was my dream. And something I feared was as equally unattainable as this house with its pretty door.

A woman patiently waited outside at the bottom of the stairs that lead to the impressive main entrance. If she didn't wear modern clothing, I might've mistaken her for a beautiful sculpture. She wore a rose-coloured dress that hugged her chest and thighs and cut off just below her knees, and matching heels with ankle clasps. The top of the dress had a boat neck that showed off her glowing brown skin, and her hair was pulled back into one of those fancy French twist styles I'd never mastered. Her whole appearance screamed refined culture, and here I was, walking up in head-to-toe leather with my black hair wrangled into a messy pony-tail and my make-up free face tattling on my complete lack of vitamin D and vacation time.

"Welcome, Lark." Her creamy, smooth voice rolled over my skin.

"Estelle?"

The woman nodded.

"You have a beautiful voice," I said. Mentally, I winced. It was an idiotic thing to say. How old was Estelle? The woman in front of me looked no more than twenty-five, but human servants could live for hundreds of years.

"Thank you." Estelle smiled, showing off beautiful white teeth. "If you'll follow me, I'll take you to Gregor."

I nodded and followed Estelle around the side of the house and past a high hedge that blocked off a section of property. I glanced over my shoulder at the house and swallowed a sigh. Guess I wasn't getting inside today. Should I be relieved or upset about that? I'd never been inside a vampire lair before and the inside of that house was probably just as pretty as the outside.

Curiosity was my greatest weakness and would ultimately be my undoing.

Estelle caught my look and smiled again. "It's a magnificent house, isn't it?"

"I was kind of hoping it would be awful."

Estelle chuckled and shook her head. "It's not. Everything Gregor purchases is tasteful and refined. It's a little annoying at times."

"So, you get it."

"Next time, I'll give you the inside tour."

Next time? Not sure I liked the sound of that. No matter how nice Estelle seemed, or how badly I wanted to peek at the interior design of the mansion, I had to remember where I was and who surrounded me. Vampires. Not just any vampires. Old and powerful vampires. The strong death magic that fuelled them swirled around this place, heavy in the air.

The path opened up to a small clearing protected by tall hedges at least fifteen feet high. In the centre of the clearing, Gregor stood with three other vampires. I recognized his companions as the same vampires that had been with him when he visited me at work. The closer I drew near, the more the death magic vibrated in the air. While Gregor's companions wore black suits, Gregor had opted for a dark navy one, paired with a floral collared shirt. He'd left the first few buttons unfastened. Designer, expensive, tasteful.

These three words seemed to describe Gregor's whole aesthetic.

But he didn't get to his position by dressing nicely and acquiring pretty things.

He reigned by spilling blood.

"Thank you for coming tonight, Ms. Morgan," he said.

"Lark is fine and you're welcome."

He nodded and turned to Estelle. "Thank you, my dear. You may return to the house."

Estelle sighed and flashed me a sympathetic smile before turning around on those stunning heels and walking away. As Estelle rounded the corner, out of view, and presumably earshot, Gregor turned back to me. "Do you remember our deal?"

"I remember a deal being offered, but not that I accepted it." I folded my arms over my chest.

His lips twitched. "Do you remember the deal I offered, then?"

"I do a raising and you clean my mother's blood."

"Yes. One raising equals one treatment."

I narrowed my eyes and scanned the clearing. My breath caught. Estelle had lied to me—at least a little. I stood in an unofficial cemetery. The death magic coming off the vampires in the clearing had masked the trickles of death coming from the ground. Dirt had been dug up and repacked in multiple locations. There had to be at least ten graves here.

No wonder death magic vibrated so potently in the air. I'd assumed it had all come from the vampires.

Tentatively, I reached out with my magic. These dead felt different, but I couldn't put my finger on why. Had they been drained of blood? I'd never raised a vampire victim before. If they existed, the vampires made sure nobody ever found them.

"One raising per treatment," I agreed. "With the promise that each treatment will be thorough and completed to the best of your ability, and with the option for me to terminate the deal without any harmful repercussions to me or those I care about."

Gregor smiled slowly.

Yeah, he knew he had me.

"And with the ability to renegotiate between raisings," I added.

Mom might only need three or four treatments of Gregor's blood to rid her of the disease rampaging through her body. Or she might need a lifetime of them.

"Those are acceptable terms. Anything else?"

"My mother's treatment must be completed within a month of the raising unless unforeseen circumstances arise, and then they must be completed at the earliest opportune time and regardless of whether something happens to me." Was I forgetting something? I'd ruminated over the idea since Gregor pitched it and thought about the conditions I wanted to place on the deal, but maybe I should've written my thoughts down. I didn't think I was forgetting anything. I'd rehearsed this part in the mirror enough times.

Gregor nodded. "You must love her very much. I agree to the terms. Is my word enough or would you like to make a blood pact?"

"I will take you on your word." Asking the Master Vampire of Victoria for a blood pact instead of taking his word would be a fatal mistake. Or at the very least, setting up our mutually beneficial relationship for failure.

Gregor chuckled and waved at the upturned earth by his feet. "I would like you to raise this one tonight."

I frowned and looked around the clearing. "I don't see a sacrifice."

Gregor tsked and shook his head. "Come, now, Lark. We both know you don't need a sacrifice."

I froze. He couldn't possibly be suggesting what I thought he was suggesting. "I can't use my own blood for summoning."

I'd learned most of what I knew about necromancy from the internet and what little information Mom could share and remember from her childhood—both her parents were necromancers. By all accounts, Mom should've been a strong necromancer, but she never touched magic and when she did, she barely managed small spells.

Sometimes, I asked Denise questions about necromancy, but she didn't have as much power as me and I remained cautious not to give away too much about my own abilities and heritage.

The man who was supposed to be my teacher disappeared just when my powers started awakening. So instead, the internet, Denise and Mom were my teachers and Mom drilled five golden rules to necromancy into me at a young age.

Never use my own blood. It would send me to the veil with no way home.

Never meet the Lord of the Veil. No one knew exactly what he was but meeting him meant death.

Never run into a barghest. The demonic guard dogs of the veil killed necromancers on sight for disrupting the balance of life.

Never reveal my lineage, specifically who my grandparents were. Mom was always vague on this rule, but it had something to do with her father having death magic and her having none—or close to none. It was unusual for two strong necromancers to have a child with little magic of their own. Maybe all the power had skipped a generation. It certainly would explain me...and Logan. Regardless, we were supposed to keep our maternal grandfather's magic a secret, but Mom refused to explain why. Maybe he'd been hiding from something or someone, and if the truth came out, they'd come for us next.

Mom's last rule was to never take more than I needed.

The idea of breaking one of the golden rules—

number one of the golden rules—sent chills running down my spine.

"That's not quite true, is it? About your blood." Gregor interrupted my thoughts. "You can use your own blood, but you don't want to," Gregor spoke slowly and patiently.

He wasn't wrong. Using my own blood carried a terrible risk, though. When I used a sacrifice, I could go to the veil if I wished and return easily, using my anchor to the blood of another. If I used my own blood, the magic sent me to the veil regardless of my wishes and left me with no anchor, no way home. I could get trapped in the veil.

When I was younger, I had made the mistake of using my own blood and my magic transported me to the veil. No amount of visualization helped me recall how I managed to get home, but I did. And I didn't care to repeat the experience just to test out whether I could do whatever it was I did again. All I remembered was unnatural wind, souls whipping by me and darkness in the distance that radiated danger and moved toward me. I blocked everything else out.

When Mom discovered what had happened, she made me swear to keep it a secret. For someone who used to come home from work and talk non-stop, Dad had gone eerily quiet after Mom told him the news. He'd disappeared from our lives shortly after that and it took me a long time to forgive myself and stop blaming myself for a grown man's actions.

"Besides, a regular sacrifice won't work for this," Gregor said.

I frowned again and studied the upturned dirt as if it would provide all the answers.

"You're not raising a corpse," Gregor said.

Oh no.

Dread clamped onto my spine as I realized what he meant before he spoke to confirm my fears. How could I be so blind? The truth was so obvious now.

"You're raising a vampire."

CHAPTER
EIGHT

I stood in the vampire's makeshift cemetery and contemplated running. Gregor promised my safety, but "safety" had a loose definition. If I raised some spirits, I might make it five steps with my death-enhanced speed and stabby stabby skills before one of the vampires pounced on me.

And if I ran now, Mom wouldn't get the treatment.

Mom needed the treatment.

And fuck it. I'd do anything for Mom.

"A vampire?" Maybe I heard him wrong. Was this even possible? Didn't they deteriorate after they died?

The three guards remained motionless. If they didn't occasionally blink, I'd suspect they were statues. What did they think about all of this?

"How much do you know about my kind?" Gregor asked.

"Besides the whole drinking blood to sustain life thing?"

His lips quirked. "Besides that."

"Not a whole lot. Sunlight is fatal, so you sleep during the day, but daytime doesn't render you unconscious. You can remain awake as long as you're not tired and not exposed to the sun."

"Imagine the surprise of the earlier vampire hunters," he said. "Hey, Esmonde?"

One of the men standing beside Gregor grunted, a smile teasing the corners of his lips.

I jerked back.

One of the minions had broken character. I hadn't expected that and glanced at the smirking guard, presumably Esmonde. "I take it things didn't end well?"

"Depends on who you ask," Gregor said. "I found it quite a delightful surprise. The hunter, not so much. At least not at first." He turned to Esmonde. "Would you agree?"

The large vampire with hazel eyes and light brown hair stopped smirking and grimaced. "I am content with my life, master."

Oh, the drama. Part of me wanted to hear more of the story, yet the other part, a much bigger and louder part, still wanted to book it out of here.

"What do you know about the making of a vampire?" Gregor turned back to me.

"There are rules about age restrictions and turning

a glamy, which is part of your role as the master vampire to oversee. You discipline other vampires for infractions on these matters." And by discipline, I meant exterminate. "Making a new vampire requires an exchange of blood, but not like the movies or romance books—one bite is not enough to turn a human. The turning process has to be intentional, but that's about all I know. Vampires are secretive about it."

"For good reason." He waved his hand at the ground. "Newly made vampires have to go to the ground to turn and they don't rise right away, leaving them vulnerable if their maker doesn't watch over them."

The reason for secrecy made sense. All it would take for a hunter to end a new vampire's life was a shovel and some sunlight.

Gregor had entrusted me with this information.

I swallowed and met his piercing gaze.

"You are trusting my word, so I am trusting you. I don't think I need to spell out the consequences for betraying my trust."

Nope. I knew the information carried a hefty price tag. If I tried to leak what I'd been told, it wouldn't be my life that paid. At least not at first. Gregor would take everyone I loved and cared for. Then he would keep me alive and torture me so I'd know the true cost of my betrayal.

He gained his position with blood, and I couldn't forget that.

I should run.

"How long do they have to stay underground?" I asked, instead. Running was out, just as saying no to the deal was off the table. Gregor might offer me safe passage home, but now that I knew more about him and the youngling vampires there'd be consequences for turning down his offer. Consequences that I'd prefer not to face, not when agreeing would also help Mom.

"Now you're asking the right questions." Gregor broke our connection to look at the clearing. "There's a direct correlation between a vampire's strength and how long they tend to stay in the ground. Most take about a year, some take less, and some take more. And some...some never rise at all."

I hesitated. Some never rose at all? They just stayed in the dirt, dead? "I'm sorry."

A vampire's progeny were akin to children, which was why a vampire didn't make the choice to turn a human lightly. To try to turn someone, to love them that much, to take their life and put them in the ground with the hope they'd one day rise, and then have them remain forever buried, would be devastating.

Gregor nodded, acknowledging my words. "Some never rise..." He looked over at me again, his brown gaze flashing with intense emotions. "Unless a powerful necromancer raises them with their own blood."

I gulped. All four vampires studied me. "What

makes you think it can be done?" I'd certainly never heard of it.

"I was raised by a necromancer." Gregor shrugged. "And I've had a necromancer work for me in the past."

Taking in his words, I tried really hard not to glance at the exit. By Gregor's own admission, necro-mancer-raised vampires were stronger than those who popped out of the dirt like daisies. If I agreed to this deal with Gregor, I'd be helping an already powerful and established necromancer-raised master vampire create an army of strong vampires just like him.

I swallowed and squeezed shut my eyes. Mom's face flashed in my mind.

Calm down, Lark.

I was raising one or two vampires at most to heal Mom, not an army.

Opening my eyes, I found Gregor studying me with that unnatural stillness he possessed.

"What makes you think I'm powerful enough to accomplish it?" I asked. I took great pains to hide the extent of my power. The world wasn't kind to those who stood out, especially if they were glamies, and most definitely if they used bad, naughty, death magic like me. I tried my best to blend in.

Doing three raisings last night had been an excep-tion, but Gregor had contacted me that night before I completed the two additional raisings. He'd reached out specifically to me and not my agency or another necromancer. He'd researched me and found what I wanted most in the world. Then he dangled Mom's cure in front of my nose like the life-giving carrot it was.

"Ah, now that's an easy question to answer," he said. "The necromancer who helped me in the past was your grandfather."

The air in my lungs whooshed out as if someone struck me hard in the chest. I hadn't expected that.

"My grandfather?" I tried to imagine a grandfather hobbling around the master vampire's estate to raise baby vampires, but the imagery was silly for two reasons—I never met any of my grandparents, and regardless of which grandfather worked for Gregor, he must've worked for him when he was young.

Both my grandfathers possessed death magic, but that wasn't common knowledge. One of them was the reason why Mom's golden rule number four existed in the first place.

I desperately wanted to ask Gregor which grandfather he'd worked with, but that question would give too much away and I couldn't afford that right now. Probably not ever.

"I didn't realize my paternal grandfather had worked for vampires," I said, hedging my bets. If Gregor had worked with Mom's dad, he might be the reason Mom never talked about her father, and why we knew very little about our maternal grandfather.

Gregor nodded. "An interesting individual."

I didn't know a lot about Dad's side of the family

either, and after Dad disappeared, I had to accept I never would. This tidbit of information did something weird to my insides. The twisting pain of regret and grief. I swallowed the emotions down.

An ugly thought crossed my mind. "Are you the reason my father disappeared?"

Gregor rocked back on his heels. "Quite the opposite. I had been monitoring him and planned to offer him a job when he went missing."

Huh. Not sure how I felt about that. My father's disappearance fifteen years ago had hurt. I'd cried. I'd raged. When I got a bit older, I'd slept with a bunch of bad boys to get over my daddy issues. But, in the end, I felt empty.

There was nothing left inside to get hurt but this talk of my father dredged up old feelings.

"So you found me." I concluded.

"We had to make sure you had the power and could be trusted. It took some time."

And vampires had time to spare.

"Okay." I swallowed again. "Seeing how you've witnessed this before and I've never raised a vampire, why don't you tell me how this is going to go?"

A gentle breeze blew through the clearing and Gregor paused to let it flow over his skin and tussle his hair before turning his razor-sharp focus on me once again. "You're going to spill your blood over Pierre's remains, whisper your incantation and pull his spirit from the veil."

"And that won't make him a floating soul or zombie?" I didn't have the patience to deal with zombies. Horror movies and popular television shows made them out to be fast or dangerous, but really, they acted like lost puppy dogs and became obsessed with their raisers.

Gregor shook his head. "His body is ready. He's a vampire. It's the mind that needs convincing, and the mind that's needed for a vampire to rise. The spirit hasn't found its way back from the veil and that's why we need you."

"And first thirst? You'll protect me from the new vampire?" When a vampire was first created, their thirst for blood was legendary. At least according to the tabloids. I'd never been present for one and I'd never been keen to add it to my bucket list. Hopefully, Gregor kept his promise and ensured my safety.

The master vampire's smile was slow. "You'll find you won't need my protection, but if you need it, you shall have it."

Okay... Gregor needed to work on his communication skills because the vagueness wasn't working for me. I opened my mouth to ask for more clarification, but Gregor interrupted.

"One more thing," he said.

I snapped my mouth shut.

"Your grandfather Ellis preferred an exchange of blood prior to raising the vampires."

I recoiled. Exchanging blood with a master vampire

created a temporary bond. It slowly faded as blood had a life cycle of its own, but as long as Gregor's blood ran through my veins and vice versa, he had power over me.

"Why would he allow that?" I asked.

Gregor narrowed his eyes. "He allowed it because a blood bond works both ways between a vampire and a necromancer. You'll have just as much power over me as I have with you. At least as far as the bond goes."

Right, because with or without the bond, Gregor could overpower me easily unless I somehow unlocked a new magical level.

"You can call me," I said. Like a servant. I didn't like the idea of going into work, day after day, let alone being at the beck and call of the master vampire. The ramifications of being tied to Gregor weren't great.

He nodded. "Which you might need if you end up trapped or lost in the veil, searching for my vampires. That is the reason Ellis wanted it."

The death magic around Gregor continued to pulse and thrum with seductive vibrations. It didn't change the entire time he spoke. When the dead tried to lie to me, the magic flared and felt stickier. I had no idea if I could detect a lie from a vampire, but the magic around him made me believe he spoke the truth.

"You said it worked both ways?" I'd never heard that before. To be fair, I hadn't heard of any of this before.

"You will be able to call me as well."

I stilled. I forced air in my lungs and tried to control my heart rate. "I guess the better question, then, is why you would allow a blood exchange?"

Gregor laughed, a surprisingly rich sound. "I'm strong enough to resist most calls and it's worth the risk. Losing my necromancer to the veil is something I'd prefer to avoid at all costs."

In other words, he considered me valuable.

I purposefully chose not to comment on his choice of words. Vampires were known for their dragon-like hoarding tendencies and possessiveness. If I worked for him, he would consider me his, no matter how sternly I corrected him.

Gregor waited while I decided what to do. On the plus side, I wouldn't have to worry about getting lost in the veil if my blood pulled me over. On the downside, Gregor could abuse the connection.

I took another deep breath. My heart rate started to slow back to its normal tempo. Gregor didn't seem like the type to purposefully endanger me. It was in his best interests to keep me happy and safe if what he said was true and the magic told me it was.

Another thought hit me. If he'd worked with my grandfather, he might be able to tell me more things about my powers. As his necromancer, he might want me to grow in power.

"Okay," I said. "Let's do the blood thing."

Gregor smiled in that slow, pleased way, again. He

stepped closer to me, bringing with him the smell of his expensive cologne.

I clicked my tongue, stepped back and held up my arm. "I trust the arm will suffice?"

Amusement flashed in Gregor's eyes, but he nodded and gathered my arm in his hands as if it were a precious offering. In a way, it was. I didn't offer my blood lightly. I wasn't one of those groupies hanging out in the vamp clubs begging for attention.

He bent and pressed his mouth to my skin, his soft full lips a seductive pressure right before he sank his fangs into my arm.

I jumped, bracing for the pain, but no pain followed the quick sharp jabs from the fangs. Instead, warmth spread through my body and made my vision swim. An ache bloomed between my legs and that kind of ache was completely wrong for my current situation.

Gregor pulled away from my arm and licked the blood from his bottom lip. His cheeks grew rosy, suffused with new energy, and his gaze flashed. If he made any comment about how I tasted, I might have to stab him.

He remained silent, though, maybe sensing the seriousness of the moment for me. I'd never offered my blood before and part of me still wanted to bolt.

Before I had any time to think harder on my life choices, I pulled my dagger from my hip sheath. The three vampire guards remained statue-still, but their attention laser-focused on me. I flipped the dagger in my palm to offer Gregor the hilt. I knew better than to come at the master vampire with the pointy end.

He plucked the weapon from my hand and ran it down his palm. I stepped in, brought his hand to my mouth and hesitated. Was I really about to do this?

Mom's sickly face popped into my mind again.

Yes. Fuck, yes. I was definitely doing this.

I lowered my mouth and sucked on the wound. The moment his blood hit my tongue, I lifted my head and dropped his hand.

His blood tasted like blood. No different than when I aggressively flossed, or the time I got sucker punched by an irate customer last year and bit my tongue. Blood was thicker than water and had a metallic aftertaste. It was how Gregor's blood made me feel that disturbed me. The second I forced myself to swallow the blood, heat exploded inside me. I staggered to the side.

Gregor reached out and caught my arm, steadying me much like Kang had when I'd overexerted myself at the crime scene.

Ugh. I wasn't a damsel in distress, dammit. I didn't faint.

Smiling politely, I pulled my arm free. Gregor's blood burned in my veins and my magic pinged along with it. Like a sixth sense, I knew if I closed my eyes or walked away, I'd instinctively know the location of the master vampire. Like being aware of where my arms and legs were, I was now acutely aware of Gregor.

And I didn't like it.

At all.

This was dangerous information to have. No one could ever find out about the bond or I'd have a big target on my back.

"The effects will fade," Gregor assured me.

And they would, but a healthy red blood cell had a life cycle of one hundred to one hundred and twenty days. Assuming vampire blood cells had the same or similar lifespan, I was looking at almost three months of Gregor-spidy-sensing.

No turning back now.

I nodded and took back my dagger. I used the tip of the weapon to point at the soil. "This one?"

"Yes, please." Gregor pulled himself upright as if the exchange of blood had no impact on him. He watched me though, studying me like a big cat studied its prey. "His name is Pierre Deveau."

I stood over the grave and cut open my palm. Pain shot through my hand. I pressed my lips closed and bit back a cry. Closing my hand into a fist, I let the blood drip onto the soil. More than a drip. Blood spurted from the wound and fell to the ground with a splatter. The vampires around Gregor stirred as if the smell of my blood woke them from a deep slumber.

Sticky death magic hummed and vibrated in the air, and a false wind rose up, one made from the movement of souls.

My blood travelled downward, saturating the soil

as gravity pulled it toward the bones beneath the surface. My magic pinged the moment my blood connected with the body. I whispered the incantation, weaving my magic through my blood and the blood-soaked soil, pushing it through the paper-thin skin of the resting vampire and into his bones.

Necromancy required three things—bones, blood, and power. The moment my magic touched the bones freshly soaked with my blood, the living realm slid away. I stood in the veil again, a wispy wasteland, full of souls and animated skeletons for the second time in two days. The eerie castle from before still loomed in the distance, but it was closer now. Its long shadows cast from the eerie glow of the veil almost reached my feet.

"Pierre Deveau, I summon you."

A low moan answered me. More souls joined in, one after another as they circled me faster and faster, leaving me dizzy and light-headed. My fingers tingled and pain exploded from the tips. My nails had grown into long, black talons, blood crusting at the base.

What. The. Fuck?

Whatever was happening to me and my fingers was not a part of the plan. I needed to get out of here. Right now.

"Pierre Deveau." I sank more power into my call.

Wind whipped over the barren wasteland and when I looked up again, the castle stood closer than before, its shadows now encasing me.

I hadn't taken a single step, yet somehow I'd moved in the veil. Or the castle moved to me.

Neither of those thoughts comforted me. Who lived in the castle? Why was it here? What did it symbolize?

"Who are you?" a man whispered. A translucent blue spectre floated closer.

Pierre.

"Your master is waiting, Pierre."

"My master..." The spectre floated closer.

"Yes. You're a vampire. It's time to rise."

The soul bobbed closer to me. "I remember... something."

"Gregor wants you to rise."

"Gregor..." The spectre pulsed, brightening. "I remember now. I couldn't find a way back."

I held my hand out and tried not to stare at my talons. "Let me take you."

The soul hesitated.

I glanced over my shoulder. The castle was even closer now. Outside the fortress, dead bodies hung from stakes, the flesh long since decomposed and leaving only bones. What would happen if the castle reached me instead of just its shadow?

"I don't have much time here," I told Pierre. "Take my hand and I'll lead you to Gregor."

"Gregor..." The soul sighed. It placed its bioluminescent hand in mine.

Pain shot through my body, and I was back to

standing in the clearing with Gregor and his three bodyguards. Instead of standing on my own, Gregor held me to his cold, hard body. His chest didn't move, and he didn't give off any heat. It was like cuddling a rock or ice cube.

My palm no longer bled. Did he heal it for me while I ventured into the veil or did his blood automatically make me heal faster? I didn't really know and frankly, that was the least of my concerns right now.

I pushed away and teetered on my feet. Holding up my hands to the light revealed normal fingernails. I would've thought I'd imagined the long, pointy black talons from exhaustion-inspired delirium, but blood still crusted along my nail beds and my hands ached.

"Did it work?" Gregor asked.

Before I could answer, the dirt near my feet moved and a low groan vibrated the ground.

"This is going to be a beautiful partnership, Ms. Morgan," Gregor said. He clicked his tongue and his bodyguards knelt by the unmarked grave. Without hesitation, they shovelled the dirt with their hands, helping the buried vampire dig his way out.

A beautiful friendship?

Hardly the words I'd use to describe what I'd just accomplished, but if it meant Mom got the treatments she needed, that was all that mattered.

From Gregor's smooth smile, he knew he had me, too.

A shudder racked my body as I watched a vampire,

little more than animated bones, pull free from the dirt. The smell of wet earth and blood surrounded me. The moon above illuminated pale skin stretched over the bones of a man who must've been at least six feet prior to his turning.

Pierre.

The vampire's name was Pierre.

The clothing he'd worn into the grave hung off his shoulders. His pants fell to the ground in tattered rags, but the large shirt hung long enough to provide some coverage. Some, not all. The knobs of his knees clicked as he turned around to face us.

I stepped backward.

Gregor reached out and steadied me with his hand on my arm, not forcing me to stay so much as ensuring I didn't fall over.

Pierre's face looked like a skull wrapped with translucent saran wrap. Thinning, greasy brown hair fell to his shoulders. His startling red gaze settled on me. "Master."

"No." I shook my head and jerked my thumb in Gregor's direction. "This is your master."

Why would he mistake me for the master vampire?

Pierre kept his gaze locked on mine, but surprisingly, he didn't lunge for me. He stood as if frozen, his eerie focus trained on me. With his mouth slightly parted, he made a low keening sound. It grew louder and louder.

I winced as the shrill volume increased.

"I thirst," Pierre whimpered.

Gregor leaned in and whispered in my ear, "I think that is your cue to leave."

"I thirst, Master." Pierre pulled at his shirt, ripping the fabric.

Death magic swirled in the air, tantalizingly close. I could reach out and pull on it, wrap it around my wrist and play with the vampire like a puppet.

Or at least try to.

The moment I touched that magic, Gregor would likely slit my throat.

Pierre started sobbing, and I looked around the clearing at the other vampires. Was no one going to help him? His death magic reached out to me, almost as if it wanted comfort. My chest constricted.

Esmonde sighed and stepped forward, the gravel churning under his expensive shoes. He shrugged out of his jacket and tossed it on the grass before rolling up his shirt sleeve. Without a word, he held out his exposed arm to Pierre. "Drink."

The newly risen vampire tore his red gaze from my face and locked his attention on the arm. With lightning-fast reflexes, he grabbed onto Esmonde's arm, opened his mouth and struck. He latched his mouth to Esmonde's skin with an audible smack and started sucking.

The other vampire stood there stoically as Pierre sucked on his arm, making loud slurping sounds. The others looked away, their lips twisted down in grimaces, while their death magic rose around them.

I'd never been around feeding vampires before and the sheer strength of magic dancing in the air was intoxicating, addictive, and tempting. So tempting. Maybe if I just brushed it with my own, I could see if—

Gregor cleared his throat. "The blood donors will arrive soon, and as much as I'm sure you're riveted with this blood exchange, you most definitely do not want to be present for what comes next."

Right. "Yeah, good point. I'll talk to you later."

Gregor chuckled and shook his head. "Until we meet again, Ms. Morgan."

I swivelled around and walked as quickly to the exit from the clearing as possible without appearing to run. I had no desire to watch a blood-feeding orgy.

"No..." Pierre whined behind me. Gravel crunched.

I resisted the urge to turn around and stepped through the break in the hedge.

"Let her go," Gregor said.

More whimpering ensued behind me, and I quickened my pace to make it back to the main building where I'd parked my car.

Let her go.

Pierre might've let me go tonight, and Gregor, too, but I had no allusions of freedom. I was truly caught and entangled in vampire business now. And I'd gladly pay the price five times over again if it meant Mom found relief from her illness.

CHAPTER NINE

I stood in the café waiting for my order to be announced. How could I be standing here, doing something so ordinary, so mundane and simple as ordering a latté when not even twenty-four hours ago, I'd agreed to work for the Master Vampire of Victoria as his blood-bonded, albeit temporary, necromancer? I now raised super-powered baby vampires at his discretion.

A shudder racked my body at the memory of Pierre's red gaze settling on me when he first pulled free of the soil with his thin skin and tattered clothes.

"Ms. Morgan? Is that you?" a man's voice snapped me out of my thoughts.

Just as well. My mind wasn't a safe place to roam right now.

I straightened and turned to find Hudson Harrison standing in the café holding a steaming takeaway cup.

"Mr. Harrison. Hello." What was he doing here? Victoria wasn't *that* small.

A line had formed along the display case of baked goods. Across from the counter, shelves lined the walls, filled with thirty-dollar mugs and cups, while pedestal tables with uncomfortable metal chairs filled the space in between. A number of people sat at the tables, but most opted to take their five-dollar blended beverage outside to enjoy the heat.

"Please, call me Hudson." He walked over to the lids, plucked one from the stack and snapped it onto his cup, the green-tea tag dangling down the side. He looked more relaxed today. Maybe I imagined it, but the tension in his face was gone. He wore fitted jeans and a baby blue cotton Henley with the sleeves pushed to his elbows to show off his tanned and toned forearms.

"I'm really glad I ran into you." He turned back to me.

"Lexa!" A barista called out. "Latté for Lexa?"

I sighed and walked up to the counter, turning my back on Hudson. "Is this for Lark, by any chance?"

"That's what I said." The barista with pink hair batted her full set of fake eyelashes at me. Her makeup was flawless, and a flash of jealousy stabbed my chest. I would never acquire that skill level. Good thing I didn't care what the spirits thought of my appearance.

Or my talons.

No amount of internet searching had provided me

with information on this new development, so I concluded the talons and the castle weren't normal and I should stick with the living realm—no more jaunts to the veil for me.

"Thank you," I said to the barista. After I snapped a lid on my drink, I picked up the takeout cup and turned to find Hudson waiting.

Why was he still here?

He offered me a small smile. "I wanted to apologize."

I rocked back on my heels. I hadn't asked that question out loud—at least I didn't think I did—but maybe my facial expression said everything for me. Logan was always telling me how I had a crappy poker face.

"Apologize?" I asked. "For what?"

There were plenty of reasons, of course, but I wanted him to clarify. Just because they were obvious to me didn't mean they were to him.

"I called you out for a job with no notice, flashed my money at you, and didn't even thank you after it was over."

Customers gawked at me. A pair of women wearing identical infinity scarves—in summer—smirked and the lecherous old man hanging out by the expensive mugs leaned in, his gaze flashing with interest.

"And now you've made me sound like a sex worker in a public place." I raised my coffee cup. "Thank you for that."

I didn't have a problem with sex workers. In fact, I had a lot in common with them. They sold their bodies, and I sold my magic. What I didn't like was being made to feel less than adequate or normal by a client in a public place because of my chosen occupation.

Probably something else I had in common with sex workers.

Hudson sighed. "I'm really messing this up. You did a fantastic job, but you were obviously exhausted, and I asked you out instead of helping. I'm sorry."

"It's fine." Everything was fine. Nothing to see here.

More people had looked up from their phones to watch the conversation unfold.

"I really would like to take you out," he said. "Lunch or dinner? Please let me make it up to you."

Dating wasn't really my thing. I didn't have the time or the energy to put into it, only to get rejected or disappointed. My work schedule and line of work automatically made me incompatible with most potential partners, anyway. Ricky never stopped complaining about my shortcomings as a partner.

Jerk.

Maybe I should've let Logan stab him when I discovered the cheating.

"Please?" Hudson asked.

"Sure." I would probably try to get out of it later, but right now I wanted everyone to stop looking at me.

He smiled. "You won't regret it."

I already did, but I bit back that reply and smiled back instead. "You can call my office and set something up."

"I look forward to it." He hesitated and checked his watch. "Unless...what are you up to right now?"

I opened my mouth to spew out some excuse when my pocket vibrated. I held up my finger and pulled out my phone. Kang's number flashed across the screen. "Sorry. I have to get this. I'll see you later."

I raised my coffee cup again in a silent goodbye and walked toward the exit before Hudson flashed me that charming schoolboy smile.

"We found the husband," Kang said by way of greeting.

I used my shoulder to push open the door and step outside. The smell of coffee and gentle sounds of instrumental music faded away, replaced with exhaust fumes and the buzz of the city.

I contemplated Kang's announcement. The detective never called me regarding investigations or to provide updates about open cases in the past. Jacobs took care of that.

"Congratulations," I managed to speak through clenched teeth. "Why are you calling me?"

"He's also dead."

CHAPTER
TEN

My knee-high black leather riding boot sank half a foot into mud. I swatted mosquitoes and small flies away from my face and attempted to pull my foot free. It might be summer, but the warmer weather had yet to dry out the denser parts of wooded areas.

The surrounding forest buzzed with life, a surprising block of green space nestled in the middle of suburbia. How long would it last before another developer got their grubby hands on this space to chop it into sections and sell it off, piece by piece, with cookie-cutter homes on each plot? Vancouver Island grew almost as fast as the housing prices.

"About fucking time, Morgan." Kang ducked under the crime scene tape. Dark circles lined the underside of his eyes, and he looked rough—hair slightly mussed, colouring paler than usual, lips pressed together.

If Kang ever stopped greeting me like this, I'd keel over from shock.

"You look..." I winced. Was it just the other day Denise had commented on my appearance? It hadn't made me feel any better.

Kang raised an eyebrow. "Like shit? Yeah, I'm aware, Morgan. Get your leather-covered ass over here and help us solve the case."

"Can you give me a hand?" I waved at my stuck boot.

Kang scowled and stepped off the path. He held out his hand and I slapped my hand in his. He hauled me out of the mud, the ground making a loud slurping sound as I pulled free. The moment I had both feet on solid dirt, Kang released my hand. His gaze dropped to my wrist and the healing bruises there. His dark eyebrows dipped down and he balled his hands into fists, but he didn't say anything else. Instead, he stepped to the side and held up the yellow tape so I could duck under.

"Thanks."

He grunted in response and ducked under the tape after me. He released the yellow crime scene tape and pointed at the tree line. "This way."

I nodded and headed toward the trees but hesitated when I drew near.

"Brace yourself," Kang leaned in to say. He placed his hand on the small of my back and guided me toward the narrow trail. "This one's...odd. He's down here."

I shivered.

Unlike Jacobs, who sounded like a broken record by this point, Kang rarely gave me a heads up.

I swallowed and took my time picking my way down the trail through the forest. Death clung to the air, and I would've found the corpse without the detective's help. The corpse's body radiated death, practically screaming its location.

I stepped onto the bank of a slow burbling brook, the ground littered with brown pine needles and damp moss. In the centre of the bank lay Mr. Darren Riley. Or at least what was left of him.

He looked like someone had vacuum-packed his bones, using his skin as the plastic wrap. Nothing of his flesh remained. His gaunt face stared up at the sky, his wide unseeing eyes protruding from his skull. Blood covered his hands, he was missing a number of fingernails, had scratches along his forearms, and his wrists had been slit. A bloody knife with bits of tissue clumped at the base of the blade lay on the ground near his body.

Darren's expression looked serene as if he'd died peacefully instead of meeting some horrific end. His blood-soaked clothes hung loosely around his skeletal limbs. The blood had dried, giving the fabric a hardened, crispy appearance.

If I didn't know he'd recently been a living, breathing, member of the human race a few days ago, I'd assume this wasn't a fresh kill. He resembled the corpses I rose for estate disputes more than the murder scenes Kang and Jacobs dragged me to.

"He had his phone on him," Kang said. "We used his thumb and face to sign in. There was a suicide letter written in an open note app."

Despite the slit wrists, this didn't look like a suicide at all. My face must've said what I was thinking because Kang elaborated.

"To summarize the note, he admitted to killing his wife but didn't say why. He tried to cut up her body to dispose of her when he became overwhelmed with disgust, regret, and grief."

"So he killed himself?" I studied the body and frowned.

"He doesn't appear to have any blood left in his body," Kang said. "But there are no fang marks."

"He's not just missing blood," I replied. "Where's all the muscle and fat? It looks like only bones and skin are left."

Did Kang know about my connection with the master vampire? Had he made that comment to imply something or warn me? Did I need to disclose that information? I paused and reviewed my agreement with Gregor. It didn't present a conflict of interest. Yet.

I glanced up at Kang to discover he wasn't watching me at all. Instead, he scanned the forest as if still looking for the murderer.

"Do you have enough to raise him?" Kang asked.

"All I need is the bones," I said. "And blood."

He nodded and waved at Detective Jacobs who waited nearby cradling a chicken.

Not wanting to prolong this part of the process any more than necessary, I relieved Jacobs of the sacrifice, murmured my incantation, and raised Darren's spirit using the death magic flowing through my veins.

Mr. Riley appeared almost right away. He hovered over his corpse, hair dishevelled and frowned. "I didn't mean to," he said.

"What didn't you mean to do?" I asked.

He ran a hand through his phantom hair. "I was so angry."

"What were you angry about?"

"Her. Life. Everything." The spirit floated back and forth as if pacing.

"Why were you angry at Addison?" I prodded.

The spirit grew more agitated, vibrating, and floating back and forth. He muttered something incoherent, but I couldn't catch what he'd said.

"Did you kill Addison?" I asked.

"I didn't mean to," he said. "I don't remember any of it."

"What do you remember?"

"When she got home, I was so angry. And the next thing I knew I was standing over her on the bed with the knife." The spirit paused and hung his head. "There was so much blood. I panicked and tried to cut her up—to dispose of her, you know? And then I thought, 'What the hell am I doing?' I was so disgusted with myself. How could I do something like that? Why would I even try to get away with butchering my own wife? I ran. I ran and ran and ran and then..."

I waited, but he didn't continue.

"And then?" I prompted.

The spirit stopped vibrating and turned to me. "And then nothing. I ran here and wrote a note to confess and apologize. I slit my wrists and everything after that is blank."

I looked over at Kang. Before I would've relayed all the information first, but now I knew he at least saw and heard the spirits. Did he want me to keep up the charade or just end this?

Kang sighed and shook his head. "We'll test the blood on his body and the weapon to confirm his story, but we have enough."

"This doesn't look like a normal suicide, Kang. I'm no doctor but losing blood doesn't usually cause instantaneous desiccation."

"I know."

Jacobs whipped his gaze between us, his brows furrowing deeper and deeper with each glance.

Instead of calling out Kang for his abilities, I nodded and released Darren's spirit.

Jacobs placed his hands on his hips and scowled. "Would someone like to fill me in?"

ELEVEN

I hit send on the email with my official report for the police and sank back into my chair. With the window to my office at Raisers open, the breeze snuck in and teased the corners of the papers stacked on my desk under a skull paperweight. The skull had been a gift from Logan for Christmas a few years ago and while it might be considered mildly inappropriate for the workplace, it was probably one of my most cherished possessions in the office.

Someone knocked on my door.

Before I could answer, the door swung open, the hinges squeaking a little. Logan and Brandon poured into my office. My twin looked like his normal roguish self—dark denim, dark fitted T-shirt, mysterious, dark blue gaze that seemed to take everything in, while Brandon looked like he'd just left the courthouse. He wore his gray suit today and had loosened the tie around his neck and unfastened the first two buttons. Their familiar colognes mixed together and washed over me.

I took a deep breath and relaxed. They smelled like home.

Brandon peered around the room and nudged Logan's shoulder with his own. "This place isn't big enough for the three of us."

Logan snorted.

"You've been here before, Brandon. Did you honestly just come over to insult my office space? We can't all be bigwig lawyers with corner offices that have a view of the harbour, Mr. Callahan."

Brandon smirked and pulled his shoulders back.

"I see." He was in a fighting mood. I snatched a pen off the top of my desk and chucked it at him.

Logan reached out and caught it in the air before it reached his boyfriend. "Before you get too stabby, we came to steal you away for lunch."

Brandon shot me his megawatt smile.

"You're lucky you're so adorable." A golden retriever would be easier to hurt, and I couldn't bring myself to even think about doing something as vile as that.

I glanced at my clock. It was seven at night, but we all held ridiculous work hours, so "lunch" was a loose term to mean the second meal of the day.

"I already had a latté," I said.

"Sparky," Logan warned. "We talked about this. Coffee isn't a meal."

"I can't believe it." I gasped. "My own flesh and blood. Uttering hurtful nonsense."

"I have to agree with him," Brandon piped up. "You've been relying on caffeine a little too much. You're going to crash."

"How dare you." I squinted at him. "You used to be my favourite."

Brandon laughed. "I'll always be your favourite."

He wasn't wrong.

"Come eat with us, Sparky," Logan said.

High heels clacking on the hardwood floor was the only warning we got before Denise popped her beautiful face into my office. "Oh, hello. Are you having a party without inviting me?"

She squeezed into the room behind Brandon, who widened his eyes.

"Hello, boys," she said. "Good to see you both again."

"Denise, please don't hit on them."

She placed a hand to her chest and gasped. "I only suggested a threesome if they wanted to broaden their horizons. I took a hint when they said no."

Logan narrowed his eyes, and I had to agree with his non-verbal reaction. She absolutely did not take the hint. At least not right away. I had to listen to her talk about how utterly good-looking the boys were and had to threaten to dissolve our friendship if she couldn't keep it together. She finally relented.

"Honestly." Denise flipped her hair over her shoulder. "That was years ago."

I opened my mouth to correct her timeline, but she spoke over me.

"Anyway, I'm here with a message." She waved a white piece of paper in her hand. "A message from Hudson." She waggled her eyebrows.

Both the boys perked up.

I groaned. Not because I was still looking for an excuse to get out of the date, but because Denise revealed this information in front of Logan and Brandon. "Why didn't his call get patched through to me?"

"He called when you were out so the front desk patched him to me not realizing it was a personal call." She squeezed between Brandon and Logan and leaned over to slide the paper across my desk. "It's his number, a time, and a place. He has good taste." She tapped the paper before straightening. "That's a five-star restaurant. Reservation only and usually booked up for months in advance."

"I don't really care about shit like that." I plucked the paper from the desk and quickly read the message.

"I'm honestly thrilled." Denise stepped back so I now had to face the three of them like some sort of interview panel. "It's about time you dusted off those coochie cobwebs."

Brandon laughed.

Logan shook his head.

"When is it?" Brandon asked.

I clutched the paper to my chest. I would take this information to the grave with—

"Tomorrow night." Denise clapped. "Our girl is finally going to get laid."

"I'll make sure Logan and I are out of the apartment." Brandon nodded. "So you can have some alone time."

"It's a first date," I huffed.

"So?" Brandon and Denise responded in unison.

Logan took the information in that serious stillness he had when his jovial mask slipped.

After Ricky, I wouldn't be surprised to find Logan splayed out on a nearby rooftop with a sniper gun ready to take out my date if he tried to hurt me. Logan might be efficient and ruthless at protecting my physical well-being, but he still hadn't figured out how to protect my heart.

When I discovered Ricky's cheating and stayed home, sobbing into my pillow, Logan had been almost as big a mess. Brandon had to convince him of all the reasons why assassinating my ex would be a bad idea.

Hopefully, Brandon wouldn't have to repeat those arguments.

"So I don't take men home after the first date," I said.

Brandon shook his head.

Denise nudged him and leaned over to stage whisper. "That's why she has so many cobwebs. She rarely makes it past the first date."

"Hey!"

Brandon nodded, his expression softening and sympathetic. "It's really quite sad."

"I'm right here, guys." I crossed my arms over my chest.

Denise turned to Logan. "I really worry about her."

My twin shrugged. "I'm oddly okay with my sister not getting railed on every date she goes on."

I flung my hands up in the air. "Are you all done, yet? Can we eat?"

Brandon perked up. "I thought you'd never ask."

"Make sure you close that before you leave." Denise jabbed her finger in the direction of the offending window. "You're wasting good air-conditioning."

CHAPTER TWELVE

Wearing my one and only little black dress, I sat across from Hudson at the table and studied the contours of his face in the flickering candlelight. Hudson had chosen an elegant fine dining establishment. The place had a quiet and intimate ambience without the edge of pretentiousness, and I found myself glad I hadn't ended up cancelling or offering a lame excuse to get out of the date like I'd originally planned.

Despite wearing an off-the-rack dress, I didn't feel out of place or outclassed and the appreciative look on Hudson's face when he first spotted me made the heels, the hour-long prep time and slipping on an impractical dress worth it. With loose sleeves that covered my shoulders, a V-neckline that stopped short of indecent, and a flowing skirt that ended just below the knees, my dress complimented my body without showing too much. I purchased it about ten years ago and wore it on first dates and to funerals. The matching black strappy heels had come from a massive shoe outlet sale about four years ago.

I kept the accessories simple—my gold family pendant around my neck and a knife in my purse. Logan made me pack a weapon "just in case." I gave up arguing with him about what he considered normal safety measures years ago.

The servers at the restaurant didn't wear white gloves or speak with fake British accents, but the food was worthy of the five-star rating. What surprised me more than the quality of the food was the quality of conversation. Hudson had charisma. He carried the conversation well and there never seemed to be a lull or awkward silence.

He flashed his pretty smile at me often and he was respectful to the servers. He wore dress pants and a white collared shirt with a subtle texturized pattern. No tie. I kept stopping myself from reaching out to touch the fabric of his shirt. It looked soft.

Maybe I shouldn't have tried to write him off so quickly. And maybe I should've run away.

We were already two hours deep into the night, and he had no red flags. After dating in Victoria for the last eon, that said a lot. Maybe not having any obvious red flags—aside from asking me out—was the new red flag.

Brandon would accuse me of self-sabotaging right about now if he heard my thoughts. Logan would just shake his head.

"So about your work." Hudson set his knife and fork down on the plate and leaned forward. An image of Mr. Riley's gaunt face flashed in my mind. The lingering taste of my delicious meal turned sour on my tongue. After filling in Jacobs on what Mr. Riley had shared with me, I'd left the crime scene. My part of the job was done, but the investigation was far from over for the detectives and I decided to get out of their way.

Aside from dealing with Kang's moods, the unfinished feeling, the lack of closure to a case, bothered me most about my role with the VicPD. Though I consulted on the cases, I never got to see the whole investigation through. Jacobs would eventually text me to let me know they caught the killer and sometimes I got to testify in court, but I always left crime scenes feeling dissatisfied, like my role in the process wasn't enough and certainly not finished.

"What got you into it?" Hudson asked.

"You could say it runs in the family."

He raised his eyebrows. "I know magic is hereditary but surely you had a choice."

Not if I wanted to pay the bills.

I lifted my glass of white wine to my mouth and took a sip.

Hudson squinted at me. "Did you ever want to be something else?"

127

"Oh, sure." I set the glass down. "All sorts of things —architect, doctor, veterinarian, professional horse jumper."

"Horse jumper? Is that what it's really called?"

"No idea. I don't know how to ride."

He laughed and leaned back in his chair. "So what happened? Why not take up riding?"

Like it was that easy or affordable.

It wasn't Hudson's fault he grew up with money, but it definitely made him blind to some of the struggles others less fortunate faced—some obvious, like not having the money to afford things, and some not so obvious, like not having the time or energy to pursue dreams because of slogging through day jobs to pay the bills.

"I grew up," I said.

He sighed and took a sip of water before placing his glass down on the table. "Reality really can be a bitch."

"I have stronger words for her, but yes. Absolutely."

He nodded thoughtfully and swirled the contents in his glass. "You haven't asked me about my mom."

I shrugged. "I signed a non-disclosure agreement."

He stopped swirling his drink and looked up at me. "I don't remember an NDA."

"You wouldn't. I signed one with Raisers. It's standard procedure. Our company respects the privacy of our clients and doesn't share details of our business dealings unless required to by a court of law."

"But it's just us."

I nodded. "Some clients don't wish to discuss raising their loved ones."

He leaned forward again, his drink forgotten, his tone a deep growl. "Am I still a client?"

"Not anymore."

His smile was slow and suggestive, and my body instantly reacted to it, warming under the attention. It had been so long since a man looked at me like that.

"How is your family?" I asked.

His gaze flashed and he straightened in his seat. "My family?"

"You mentioned your siblings at the raising, and how the money would help them. They must be relieved to have their financial burdens lightened." I certainly would be.

"They will be relieved," he said. "I haven't retrieved anything, yet."

"Why not?" Was it illegally obtained? Where had his mom said it was again? She'd rambled off an address and said it was in the backyard. How big was the backyard? How would Hudson know where to look? Had she been vague to protect the information from me or to make it more difficult for Hudson to find? She'd certainly found a way to slip around my control.

But regardless, Hudson didn't seem concerned

about locating the money, so why would he delay retrieving it to help his siblings? Why would he need the money to help his siblings when he already appeared to have quite a lot of his own? I definitely only had part of the story, but it was a murky area. I wasn't the police. This was our first date. I didn't want to pry, but I was also dying of curiosity and wanted to ensure I wasn't setting myself up for dating another loser like Ricky.

"I see you're confused. I'm not waiting because I want to. There's some red tape to dig in that location. If I'm too obvious about it, others will realize what I'm after."

"Ah. And I'm guessing you're not the only one looking?"

He nodded. "As far as I know, we're the only two who know the location. I don't want to hire any crews either, so after I get things sorted out, I'm going to have to dig it out myself."

I raised my eyebrows.

"I work out, but digging isn't something that I can do quickly," he explained.

"I could help." The words escaped my mouth before I had a chance to think them through. Help? Really? I refused to take any jobs that required digging out graves. I hated manual labour. I only worked out and let Logan train me how to fight because I realized the practicality of learning how to defend myself six years ago. Why would I offer to help Hudson?

Obviously, I was an idiot.

Hudson flashed me that brilliant smile again and the reason why became abundantly clear. I'd always been a sucker for a nice smile and solving mysteries.

"I'd like that very much," he said.

CHAPTER THIRTEEN

Hudson walked up to my apartment's front door with me, our hands linked together. By this point, butterflies danced in my belly. After Ricky, I'd been turned off the whole dating thing. Men kind of sucked, and though I knew not all men sucked, the ones that tended to ask me out certainly did. If anything proved sexuality wasn't a choice, it was the continued existence of heterosexual women like myself. If I had a choice in what I liked, I wouldn't be dating men at all.

Hell, I probably wouldn't be dating period.

It had been so long since I had a pleasant evening out with a man, so long since I craved the touch of another person. I wanted to invite Hudson up and find out what else his mouth could do other than smile, but I'd also just met him. If he liked me, he could wait a little longer.

I slowed down to dig my keys out of my purse and my phone buzzed. Normally, I'd ignore it, but I caught Kang's name on the screen.

With a groan, I pulled out my phone and flashed Hudson an apologetic smile at the same time. "I'm sorry. This is work."

He pressed his lips together before giving me a no-tooth smile.

Not the best sign, but the sooner he realized my ridiculous schedule and decided whether he wanted to be a part of it, the better. I refused to pretend I worked a regular nine-to-five. Not only would that be misleading, but in the past, it always ended in heartbreak.

I accepted the call. "Hey."

"Hey." Kang's deep voice rumbled through my phone.

"Do you need privacy?" Hudson asked, shifting his weight from foot to foot.

I looked over and shook my head. Kang was usually brief on these calls. In fact, he normally didn't bother with a greeting at all unless swearing counted.

"Who's that?" Kang asked.

"My date."

"I see," his tone was clipped.

"It's Saturday night, Kang. I know crime doesn't sleep, but I do. What's up?" Oh god. The last thing I wanted to do was drag myself to another crime scene.

"I just thought you'd like to know that the lab

results came back. They confirmed the blood on Darren and the knife matched Addison's."

"Oh. Okay. That's good right?" He never shared details about an active case. As far as he was concerned, I was on a need-to-know basis and I didn't need to know anything other than the victim's name.

"Yeah, it's good. It solves Addison's murder, but I'm not convinced this is a murder-suicide. I mean, you saw the body."

I certainly did and I agreed with Kang. "I'm not sure how I can help you prove otherwise," I said. "But thank you for letting me know about the labs."

Kang grunted something close to a goodbye and hung up.

"Everything okay?" Hudson asked. He looked so clean cut and just...normal, standing on my apartment's landing. The most bizarre and out of mainstream thing he'd probably ever done in his life was hire me. And the second thing was probably asking me out on a date.

Hudson contrasted with my world and was the exact opposite of almost every guy I'd dated in the past.

Maybe that was why I found him so appealing.

"Everything is fine," I said. "Just one of the detectives I work with following up on a recent case."

Hudson's eyebrows rose almost all the way to his hairline. "You live an exciting life."

I shrugged. What could I say to that? It was exciting and also exhausting.

Hudson smiled and stepped closer. He hadn't left. He hadn't run away at the first phone call during a date. The butterflies returned.

"Thank you for dinner. I had a great time," I said.

His smile widened and he leaned down. He was going to kiss me. Finally. I closed my eyes and tilted my chin up, my skin warming already at the promise of connection, of touch, of something I'd been deprived of for so long.

"Ms. Morgan?" A familiar voice called out from the street. The rumbling sound sent ice down my spine and acted like a bucket of water being dumped on my libido.

I stiffened and Hudson quickly straightened to turn to the speaker.

Gregor stood on the sidewalk in front of my apartment building wearing a dark gray designer suit and a pin-striped shirt. The outfit probably cost more than my car. His black hair fell in soft curls to his jawline and shone under the overhead streetlight. His face was paler than I remembered it, or maybe it just seemed that way tonight in contrast to the warm-blooded man standing a foot away from me.

"Gregor. You have the most unfortunate timing," I said. The heat from the anticipation of a kiss had fled, leaving me cold and cranky.

The master vampire dipped his chin as if to concede my point. "My apologies, Ms. Morgan. I found myself arriving at an awkward time and felt you'd prefer me to interrupt now than to stand to the side as a spectator and interrupt later."

He had a point.

"Gregor?" Hudson's eyes widened and he kept whipping his head back and forth to watch me and the vampire speak. "Gregor Fissore, the Master Vampire of Victoria?"

Gregor grinned and preformed a perfect court bow. "The one and the same. And who might you be?"

Oh, hell no. I stepped forward and slightly in front of Hudson. "He's my date, Gregor. Leave him alone."

Hudson probably wouldn't be anything more than a first date now that he'd been introduced to the craziness that was my life. First Kang, now Gregor. The night couldn't get any worse.

Gregor recoiled and clicked his tongue at me as if he were insulted.

For all I knew, he'd run a background check on Hudson and probably have him followed. What lengths would the master vampire go to in order to protect his asset? To protect me?

Before I could say anything more, a cab pulled up to the curb behind Gregor. The rear door opened, and my brother's boyfriend tumbled out of the vehicle. He grunted on impact with the sidewalk, pulled himself up and turned to offer his hand to Logan. My brother made a lewd comment about Brandon's ass in the air that even made me blush and I lived with them.

Brandon laughed, a loud hysterical bark of a sound,

and hauled Logan from the cab's backseat. They stumbled along the sidewalk, arms over each other's shoulders, giggling like schoolgirls, and completely oblivious to their audience.

A smile spread across my face.

No one would know from looking at them that Logan was one of the city's most lethal assassins, and Brandon held some sort of record for throwing people in jail. Brandon often joked that we should start a family business—Logan would kill them, I'd raise them, and Brandon would make sure everyone stayed out of jail.

Sometimes, the thought was incredibly tempting.

The boys paused to check out Gregor's ass and my brother, my fucking brother, piped up to say, "Hello, daddy."

That elicited joyous laughter from Brandon as he pulled Logan in to lay a loud, wet kiss on his cheek, either out of affection or because he was already falling into him. Hard to tell. They stumbled past the master vampire and up the stairs.

I loved Logan and Brandon, and while I was glad they were cutting loose and having a great time, their timing was atrocious. I wanted to be desirable to Hudson, and professional with Gregor, and I didn't want either of them to meet my family. And now they both got a sneak peek into my personal life and two of the three people I loved most in the world.

Gregor's smile was positively predatory. His gaze

flashed with amusement, and he tracked my brother and his boyfriend up the stairs.

Oh, hell no times two. Logan and Brandon might joke around and flirt, but they were in a committed serious relationship. Not even Gregor fucking Fissore could ruin that.

Logan spotted me first. "Sparky, baby. You should've come out with us tonight."

I mentally slapped my forehead. This was my life.

"Thanks again for tonight," I said to Hudson. "I had a great time."

He closed his mouth and slid his gaze away from Logan and Brandon to meet mine.

"It's probably best if you go now while you can," I continued.

He laughed and shook his head. "See, you lead an interesting life."

"That's one way to describe it."

"I'll call you." He leaned down and kissed my cheek before sauntering down the stairs.

Brandon and Logan exchanged polite greetings with Hudson on the stairs before Hudson left down the sidewalk to where he'd parked the car. The boys both turned to check him out as he walked by.

They weren't even trying to be subtle.

Thankfully, Gregor stayed where he was, observing the scene like a cinematic production.

Brandon recovered from studying Hudson's ass first and turned to give me two thumbs up and a wink.

"Damn, Sparky," Logan whistled. "That's some nice corporate ass."

I rolled my eyes and jerked my chin toward Gregor. "If you two could get inside before you start dishing out all my life quirks and secrets, I'll go speak with Gregor. I'm quite certain the master vampire didn't travel all this way to watch the soap opera of my life."

"Actually, I'm quite enjoying this," Gregor called out.

I squinted at him. Did he just make a joke?

Logan and Brandon finally stumbled up the last of the stairs to reach me on the landing outside the double doors to the apartment building.

"Sparky." Brandon laid his hand on my shoulder. "Don't take this the wrong way, but your life is far from exciting enough to be a soap opera."

Logan winced and nodded.

"Romantic comedy?" I asked.

They shared a look before answering in unison. "Horror."

"Ugh." I waved my hand in the air at them as if it would somehow banish their attitude and left them to figure out how to unlock the door in their current drunken state. I walked down the steps and approached Gregor. What did he want anyway? Hadn't he heard of phones?

Gregor leaned to the side to look over my shoulder

to where the boys cursed and shoved at each other. "You're not going to help them?"

"No." I flipped my hair off my shoulder. "They're grown adults and after that horror comment, they deserve every second of frustration."

Though Brandon and Logan were laughing and having a great time, I had no doubt the dark presence that lurked deep in my twin's psyche watched me and my interaction with Gregor. If I needed help, Logan would be clutching Gregor's shirt with a dagger to his throat faster than I could draw the small knife in my purse. Some part of Logan always watched over those he loved. He didn't need my help with the door.

Gregor chuckled, the moonlight reflecting in his dark gaze. "I had a sister once."

His mouth turned down for the briefest of moments, revealing a small peek into his sadness and past. Denise always said vampires lived long lives if they survived the politics. Gregor had definitely lived a number of lifetimes. A lot of people glorified the extended lifespan for the opportunities to make money and experience more of what the world had to offer. They conveniently forgot all the heartache that came along with it, all the goodbyes.

Mom always said you couldn't get something for nothing, and that included vampirism.

"Did you need something?" I asked. "Or did you just come by to chat?"

He smiled slowly, as if reading through my

abrupt change in topic. Maybe it was rude of me not to ask about his sister, but that sad look made me think he might not welcome my questions. He probably hadn't meant to make the comment in the first place.

"I'd like you to speak with Pierre," he said.

"Pierre?" I raised both my eyebrows at the mention of the vampire I'd raised the other night. "Why? Is he okay?"

Gregor waved his hand in the air in a dismissive way. "He's fine."

I resisted the urge to clutch my skirt or tap my strappy heels on the pavement. "Then why do you need me to speak with him?"

"You raised him."

"On your request..." Why had he said that with an accusatory tone? What was I missing? I personally despised conversations like this—the ones where I felt like I was doing all the work, where every question was answered with single words or short sentences, forcing me to ask more to figure out what the fuck was going on. The older I got, the less patience and tolerance I possessed.

Gregor started walking down the sidewalk, making me choose between defying the Master Vampire of Victoria or following him.

I glanced up at the main entrance of the apartment building where the boys still giggled. With his uncanny senses, Logan looked up and met my gaze, his lifted brow a question. I jerked my chin up to assure him I was fine, and he nodded.

At least I thought I'd be okay.

Maybe I was being a little presumptuous.

Taking a deep breath, I took a few quick steps to catch up and walk beside Gregor. My heels clacked along the sidewalk and echoed into the night.

"Have I done something wrong?" I asked.

"When you raise a spirit and push the essence into its decaying body to reanimate the corpse, why doesn't the zombie run off and start eating brains like they do in all those horror movies?" he asked.

I frowned, not understanding where he was going with this. "Well, they could if I lost control."

"But they don't. Why?"

"Because I can control them..." A headache bloomed behind my eyes. What was he trying to suggest? "Are you trying to tell me I can control Pierre now?"

"That's what I wish to find out."

I swallowed. Wouldn't he already know? He'd worked with my grandfather after all. "And if I can?"

"You will order him to obey me," he said.

"And if I don't? If I can't?"

"I will ensure you obey me."

CHAPTER

FOURTEEN

I sat on the leather seat inside the quiet Town Car, muscles tight, trying to replay events in order to figure out where I went wrong. With my legs crossed at the ankles, I smoothed down my dress to make sure I didn't unintentionally flash the Master Vampire of Victoria my lace panties. My dress fell below my knees standing, so the action and the worry were completely unnecessary, but it didn't stop me from going through the motions anyway.

I felt like I was back in high school, sent to the principal's office and left to sit outside so I could think about what I had done. Flashbacks of my youth bombarded my mind. I'd sit for an hour in the waiting area of the main office that smelled like paper, staples and teen spirit, and think about all my possible transgressions, only to learn they'd called down the wrong

Morgan twin. Logan would find everything hilarious and wink as he passed me in the office, while I talked myself down from a panic attack and wiped the cold sweat from my brow.

Except this time, I knew there'd been no mistake. Logan wouldn't magically appear with his wide, shit-eating grin and tell me to relax.

Maybe agreeing to go with Gregor hadn't been such a great idea. But we'd exchanged blood. He could find me anywhere and he could try to use the temporary bond to force my compliance. Running was always an option, but I'd have to take Logan and Brandon with me and they were probably still giggling uncontrollably like two school kids outside the apartment building.

"Nice necklace." Gregor broke the silence to nod at my chest.

I plucked the pendant up and studied it under the flickering light flooding the cabin as we passed the street lights. An engraved head of a griffin chomping on a human skull decorated the centre of the circular pendant. "Thank you."

"Family heirloom?"

"In a way. My father had one like it and got two identical ones made as a gift for me and my brother."

"What does it symbolize?"

I shrugged and released the pendant, letting it fall. "My father disappeared before he could explain it. All I know is that it's a family thing. Our last name is

Welsh." I clamped my mouth shut as Mom's voice lecturing me to keep my family history private popped into my mind.

"A descendent of Morcant." Gregor flashed me a small smile.

I straightened in my seat. The word Morcant was engraved on the back of the pendant.

"I'm aware of the origins of your surname, Ms. Morgan. I'm also aware that most people accept the translated meaning of Morcant from Welsh to mean 'sea circle' or 'sea defender' in English."

"But not you?"

His smile grew. "Not me. I've been around long enough to know of the connection between Morcant and the Morrigan. The name is not referring to the literal ocean so much as a sea of spirits."

"The veil," I whispered.

"Exactly." He leaned back in his seat "Your grandfather also had an identical pendant."

"What happened to him?" I asked. Mom didn't know and Dad would never say. I always figured I'd get the truth out of him one day, but then he disappeared and now that one day would never happen.

"Your grandfather?" Gregor lifted a dark brow. "What happens to most powerful necromancers, I suppose. Ellis went to the veil one night and never returned."

I shivered. Had my father met a similar fate?

The driver pulled up to Gregor's mansion and Estelle stood outside waiting for us. Did Gregor somehow message her telepathically or had she waited this whole time?

I glanced at Gregor. He met my gaze with an impassive expression as if the conversation about my family history hadn't happened at all. He waved at the door. "After you."

I slipped from the car before the driver could jog around to my side of the vehicle.

"Good to see you again, Ms. Morgan," Estelle said, voice as smooth as silk.

"Lark is fine."

Estelle's smile widened. She was wearing one of those power suits, the fashionable kind with wide shoulders and pants that tapered to the ankles with a flowy type of material. The blue colour made her skin glow and she'd paired the outfit with gold accessories and matching strappy heels.

I suddenly felt very underdressed even though I wore the fanciest thing I owned.

"Do you always look so nice?" I asked.

"Of course," Estelle said. "Why would I want to spend eternity looking less than my best?"

I shrugged. Maybe I'd never understand what it was truly like to be a vampire, or a human servant, because if I had to wear heels for an eternity, I'd probably stake myself. All I wanted to do right now was sleep.

And sleep was one of the three big things that scared vampires.

Sun, sleep and stakes.

Of course, no one tried to stake vampires anymore. The weapon was unreliable at best and superior weapons existed to kill off the blood suckers nowadays. But none of the other weapons had quite the same ring to them.

"Come." Estelle gently grabbed for my hand and placed it on her arm. "I'll take you to see Pierre."

With no polite way of avoiding the house—aka the death trap—I followed Estelle to the front doors. I mean, it was a little late to look for an out, anyway. I was here, surrounded by vampires. Though Estelle was a paragon of manners, I didn't really have any viable choices other than accepting her offer.

I might be at a disadvantage, but that didn't mean I was without means to defend myself. With so many vampires around, death magic coiled around me. I pulled it to my skin, just in case. I'd never practiced using my magic on vampires, but I wasn't above trying. If I walked into a trap, I wouldn't go down without a fight. Fuck morals and legislation.

Estelle turned to face me before opening the doors. "I told you I'd give you a tour the next time."

I made a non-committal sound. Too aware of Gregor at my back and his guards closing in behind me, I wasn't exactly feeling like a tour.

Estelle's eyelashes fluttered and she flicked an

annoyed glance over my shoulder. "What did you do to her?"

"Nothing, my pet," Gregor's smooth voice wound around me.

Estelle narrowed her eyes at the master vampire.

He made a sound, something between a grunt and a snort.

"Her heart is beating twice as fast, Gregor." Estelle's tone was flat. How would she know? Did human servants pick up other glamy abilities in addition to a longer lifespan?

"I made sure she understood the stakes of tonight's visit," he said.

Stakes? Hah! Interesting choice of words.

"So you threatened her?" Estelle asked, her tone sharp.

"*Chouchou*," Gregor's voice pleaded. Of course, he'd have an adorable French nickname for Estelle.

Wait. "I thought you were Italian?"

Gregor paused and flicked his gaze to me. "And being Italian excludes me from using a French term of endearment for my French human servant?"

"Err..." I looked away from his intense expression.

"I lived in France for hundreds of years," he added. "Longer than I'd ever stayed in Italy."

Estelle pushed the door open. "I apologize for the circumstances that brought you here, Lark. Of course, a tour is the last thing you want right now," she spoke over her shoulder. "We'll get this Pierre nonsense out of the way first and then, depending on how you're feeling, we can do the tour after."

I nodded even though I walked a few steps behind Estelle and there was no way for her to see me. Pretty sure I wanted to go home straight after this and jump into my pajamas.

We moved in a silent procession through the house, Estelle's tasteful heels clicking and clacking in staccato with mine. The boots and shiny shoes of Gregor and his goons hit the floor with leisurely, soft gaits. No stomping, no slapping, no rush or tension.

Just another night in the eerily quiet vamp house.

This better not become a regular experience for me. My blood pressure couldn't take it.

Estelle finally stopped outside a set of wood-panelled doors and stood to the side. She reached forward, turned the knob and pushed the door open. "You will be okay, Lark Morgan."

Estelle's confidence wasn't infectious, at least not for me, but I appreciated the effort she made to put me at ease. Flashing her a smile, I stepped into the room.

An intricate executive desk sat in front of a large, panelled window. Each side of the room bore dark oak bookshelves filled with books, and the place smelled of old paper, dust and a hint of vanilla, which seemed odd. I had a hard time envisioning vampires in a bath and body store sniffing the fragranced candles.

Pierre stood in front of the desk and turned at my entrance. His eyes widened before shifting to look at

Gregor who stepped up beside me. Pierre looked better than he had the other night. Not nearly as gaunt, his face had a more fleshed out appearance and rosy cheeks. He wore simple jeans and a T-shirt and from the awkward loose fit, they either belonged to someone else or they'd been purchased quickly without a fitting. They were clean, though, and a huge improvement on the tattered remains he'd worn when he first emerged from the grave. Instead of red eyes like he'd had when he rose from the ground, he settled a light brown gaze on me, the almost golden colour had a startling impact. He'd washed his long brown hair and it fell to his shoulders in soft waves.

"Command him." Gregor jerked his chin in Pierre's direction.

Pierre licked his full lips, his gaze nervously bouncing between the two of us.

"To do what?" I asked.

"Anything. The more absurd, the better, because you'll know it's your compulsion doing it," Gregor said. With a flat tone and a blank expression, it was impossible to know exactly how he felt about this situation, but if I had to guess, I'd say displeased.

I turned back to Pierre. "Sorry about this."

Pierre smiled, flashing white fangs, but his gaze remained soft. "You led me out of the veil, *ma belle*. You have nothing to fear from me."

Okay, then. I might be shaking and silently

freaking out, but I definitely liked the French nickname.

"I'd like you to kneel before me and confess your undying love," I said.

Gregor barked out a laugh.

Pierre shook his head. He leaned against the desk and folded his arms.

"Put some magic into it this time," Gregor suggested.

I sighed, rather unsure I quite knew how to do as he suggested or whether I wanted to succeed at this. I wrapped my magic around my words and spoke again as if I spoke to a reanimated corpse. "Kneel before me."

Pierre lurched from the table and stumbled forward. He tripped, fell, and still kept coming, crawling on the floor on his hands and knees until he reached my feet. His gaze vacillated between surprise and defiance, but he only stopped when he was on in his knees in front of me.

"I am so sorry," I whispered.

He sighed and shook his head again. "And as I said before, ma belle, you have nothing to be sorry for. You were the light that brought me out of the darkness."

We shared a smile and some of my fear eased away.

"As touching as this is," Gregor said. "I need you to release your control on Pierre."

"Sure." I turned to the master vampire. "How do I do that?"

"You order him to obey me."

I frowned, pausing long enough to glance at Pierre. He should have a say in this matter. "Shouldn't I tell him he's free or to obey himself?"

Everyone in the room stiffened.

"Ma belle," Pierre said. "No."

My confusion must've been evident on my face because Pierre spoke again. "I'm a new vampire. I need to serve a master until I can control my own impulses. This is as much for my safety as it is anyone else's."

"If you say so." He couldn't exactly tell me otherwise in front of Gregor, anyway, but knowing little of vampire ways, I had to assume he spoke the truth. I wouldn't risk my life or that of my family's to take the moral high ground that might not even exist.

I turned to Gregor. "You worked with my grandfather before. Did you have the same issue?"

"No."

"Then how did you know to check? I have nothing to hide, but why didn't you get me to do this when I raised Pierre?" And why did I feel like there was a lot more going on here and I was only privy to the bare minimum?

"I didn't realize you were that much stronger than your grandfather. It wasn't until Pierre resisted my orders that I grasped what had happened. I know your father and your father's father were both necromancers, but if I had to guess, I'd say you received power from both sides of your family. Your blood tastes of power."

He waited expectantly and a cold shiver raced along my skin. I didn't owe Gregor my pedigree and Mom had always cautioned me about revealing anything about her father.

"My maternal grandmother was also a necromancer," I said. This was common enough knowledge and something he'd discover if he dug a little. Hopefully, throwing him a bone would prevent him from trying to dig up anything more.

Gregor nodded and waved his hand at the kneeling vampire. "Please make the order."

Yeah. I had no wish to prolong this moment, either, but part of me wanted to know what orders Pierre had resisted. Had he balked because of heinous commands or because he was lost in a feeding frenzy without control? Wrapping my magic around my words once again, I spoke the words quietly. "Pierre Deveau, you will obey Gregor."

The vampire kneeling before me relaxed, the tension around his shoulders easing away.

"You may rise and attend to your affairs, Pierre," Gregor said. "Do not leave the property and do not go to a human without one of us with you."

Pierre stood and nodded at Gregor. Instead of leaving right away, he reached forward to take my hand and bring it to his mouth. He pressed his cold lips to my knuckles and the contact sent a chill down my spine.

"My deepest thanks, ma belle," he mumbled into

my hand. "Should you need something, anything, please do not hesitate to call on me."

He released my hand and walked from the room, the soft vanilla-scented air flowing in his wake.

Two seconds later, Estelle popped her head in. She must've been waiting outside. "Can we do the tour now?"

I really wanted to go home and sleep for a million years, but the immediate threat to my life had apparently disappeared and I didn't want to insult Estelle. I needed to act as if this were all normal and I wasn't fazed about anything, when really, my mind reeled, and I wanted to go home and cuddle my cat.

"I hope so." I looked over at Gregor.

He nodded.

Of course, he'd let me go, he already knew he could control me. He knew who made up my family and where they lived. I'd do just about anything to protect them, and he knew that, too. Gregor had spent serious time learning about my life.

Or maybe not. I wasn't that complex.

"Before I go on the tour, can I ask you something?" I turned to Gregor.

He frowned but didn't say no.

"Do you know anything about a suspicious death? Looked like a murder-suicide, but the husband was completely drained of blood, and that COD doesn't quite scream suicide."

"COD? Cause of Death?" Gregor narrowed his eyes. "Are you accusing me of something?"

"Definitely not. I don't think a vampire killed the victim—no bite marks. Both wrists were slit, but the victim was missing more than just blood. Nothing was really left of him besides his eyes, bones and skin. I wanted to know if you knew of anything that could kill someone in that way." I left some of the details out. In truth, I shouldn't be sharing this much about an active investigation, but if the police cases had a glamy link, Gregor might possess information crucial to solving the mysterious deaths.

Gregor tapped his chin, his frown deepening. "I had nothing to do with this death, nor do I believe any of my people were involved. If another creature is capable of killing in this manner, I am not aware of it, but I will think on the matter."

"Thank you," I said. "I appreciate any information you can pass along."

There. I did my good deed for the police tonight and didn't appear to have pissed off Gregor too much by asking.

Gregor nodded and I turned to walk away from him and his bodyguards to make my way to where Estelle waited.

What Gregor didn't realize was I'd already learned something else tonight—not about the police case, but about vampires. Something Gregor didn't know or didn't want to give away. I'd used my magic to compel

Pierre, but it wasn't because I had a bond with him from the raising. I knew what a bond with a zombie and a reanimated corpse felt like—the pull of tethering. That didn't exist between me and Pierre, not before or after I used my magic. Which meant only one thing.

I could control vampires with my death magic.

And this little tidbit might very well be my death sentence.

FIFTEEN

Denise pushed the little plate with the last sushi roll toward me and placed her other hand on the flat of her belly. "I can't."

I grinned and plucked the dynamite roll from the plate, dipped it into my wasabi loaded low-sodium soy sauce and stuffed the roll in my mouth.

Perfection.

The Japanese restaurant was tucked around the corner from the downtown restaurants lining Wharf Street. The warm air laced with smells of green tea, seaweed and rice vinegar surrounded me like a familiar embrace.

"I still say it's an abomination to soy sauce everywhere to mix in the wasabi," Denise said, raising her cup to her lips to take a sip of tea.

"Bite me."

"You're not my type."

Only necromancers would go out for sushi at one in the morning like it was a lunch date. We made plans to have late night sushi at least once a week. Because our schedules fluctuated so much with work, the day of the week and time always moved around, but we made it work. If anyone understood the crazy hours I worked, it was another necromancer.

"You know you're supposed to put the wasabi on the roll, not mix it into the soy sauce, right?" Denise raised an eyebrow and glanced at the foldable panels that separated us from the other guests.

"Mmhmm." I continued to chew the delicious roll, enjoying the nasal cleansing tingle the wasabi invoked.

"And you're not supposed to shove the whole thing in your mouth at once." Denise picked up her cup full of green tea.

I swallowed the food and smiled. "So you keep telling me. Not sure what made you an expert, but I'm going to ignore the advice."

Denise narrowed her eyes at me over the rim of her teacup before taking another sip.

"You'd think after, what, six years of friendship you'd give up that battle and accept me for my evil soy sauce and wasabi mixing ways."

"I'm stubborn like that," she said.

That was putting it mildly.

"Wait a minute." Denise narrowed her eyes. "We've known each other for seven years."

"Yeah, but I didn't like you right away."

Denise's mouth dropped open and her gaze rounded.

I pointed my chopsticks at my friend and opened my mouth to begin truly taunting her when my phone rang,

Kang's name popped up on the screen.

Denise leaned over and glanced at my phone. "Hot cop sure seems to be calling you a lot these days."

"He's not a hot cop." I stared at his name while I contemplated answering. I enjoyed working as a consultant with the police, but I also knew answering this call would mean an end to my sushi date with Denise. "He's a pain in the ass."

Denise snorted. "He could be a pain in—"

"Please, don't."

Denise shrugged.

"I don't think of him like that."

"Your loss. What do you think of him as, then?"

"A grumpy, overworked detective in serious need of sensitivity training." I accepted the call. "Hello, Kang."

"Morgan." He sounded tired, his voice lower and more growly than usual. "We have another case."

He wouldn't call me for a simple murder case. There had to be more to it.

"It's like our last one. Mentally prepare yourself."

My eyebrows shot up. "That a fact or a hunch?"

"I'll text you the address. When you get here, you'll see."

I STEPPED from the cab and took a deep breath to shake away the awful feeling of déjà vu. I faced another cookie-cutter home in an affluent suburb within the Greater Victoria area. This was a slightly older neighbourhood compared to the last one. The houses hailed from the mid-90s, all with the same light pinky-beige stucco exterior. White fences lined the sidewalk and the streetlights shone down on the road, creating little halos of light. The moon had made an appearance as well, and minus the crime scene, this would be a beautiful, late summer evening, perfect for a stroll around the neighbourhood.

The smell of freshly cut grass filled the air. Insects buzzed and the murmur of conversation flowed around me as I ignored the wide-eyed neighbours to duck under the crime scene tape and check in with the officer. I knew this one. Officer Daniels worked a lot of cases with Kang and Jacobs.

"Hey, Ms. Morgan." He dipped his chin. If someone took a picture of him, he could easily model for a police magazine cover or one of those calendars that helped raise funds for dog rescues during the holidays. Daniels had the stereotypical "good guy" good looks that the police department's publicity team often used for media. Thick black hair, chiselled bone structure, strong jaw, cleft chin, a strong brow, beige skin and piercing blue eyes that matched his uniform. A lot of people drooled over the young, healthy and fit Officer Daniels.

Not me.

The polite, considerate and all-around lovely human being wasn't my type. It was almost as if he wasn't damaged enough for me. Too clean. Too bland. Too good-looking. Despite the cut of his features, he didn't have an edge to his personality.

And yeah, I had issues.

"Hey, Officer Daniels," I greeted him. "You know you can call me Lark, right?"

He turned the clipboard toward me so I could sign in. "I know, ma'am, but I'll call you Ms. Morgan all the same."

I sighed and handed the pen back. "Is it bad?"

Daniels visibly swallowed.

"I'll take that as a yes."

He nodded and took a second before responding. "The entrance is along the side. The deceased lived in the basement suite with her fiancé."

"Has the fiancé been located?"

"No, he hasn't. We're on it though." He stepped to the side to allow me to access the path.

Without anything else to say, I nodded and made

my way to the side entrance. A lot of young couples rented in Victoria. The whole province had a housing crisis. The current market prices prevented anyone from buying except those with a lot of cash or with families willing to foot the bill.

Hell, Logan and I had well-paying jobs. But even if we didn't divert the majority of our funds to help pay for Mom's experimental treatments not covered by provincial healthcare, we wouldn't be anywhere close to saving a deposit for a house, townhouse or condo.

At this rate, I might be a renter for life. The only other option was moving somewhere else with more affordable houses.

But I'd never leave Logan, Brandon or Mom.

Ever.

I shook away the feelings bubbling up from my stomach. An active crime scene wasn't the place to dredge up uncomfortable emotions or financial planning. I needed to stay focused.

Starting with one foot, and then the other, I slipped plastic booties over the treads of my own footwear and walked inside the house.

The smell hit me first.

A fresh crime scene didn't smell as disgusting as a lot of people assumed, not unless the victim or victims had soiled themselves or the digestive tract was punctured. This was mainly due to not enough time elapsing for anything to decompose. So unless other factors were involved, fresh crime scenes like the one I

DEATH MAKER

was about to walk into smelled like fresh meat. A heavy iron smell clung to the air.

I'd worked in a butcher shop once when I was in high school. The smells were very similar.

Taking a deep breath, I turned the corner into the hallway and followed the sound of crinkling plastic.

The master bedroom was at the end of the hallway, past a simple bathroom, and a spare room that looked like it was used as a junk drawer for the household. A crime scene technician wearing full forensic coveralls took samples from the floor while detectives Kang and Jacobs stood by the entrance surveying the blood bath. A sheet partially covered the remains of a woman in a crumpled position in the corner of the room by the bed. A slender forearm with a ring and a dainty bracelet had slipped out from under the cover.

I stopped behind the detectives, but only because I couldn't move around them.

"I see what you mean," I said.

Neither of the men jumped. They turned around, stoic expressions in place. An outsider would describe them as cold or unfeeling, detached. I knew better. They were both steeling themselves from feeling too much. These kinds of scenes had a way of building up on detectives. They weren't sociopaths, they felt emotion, so they had to learn early on how to compartmentalize. This scene had smacked them hard.

"We got here within ten minutes of the call," Jacobs said. "Blood was still running down the wall."

"And we were still too fucking late," Kang's voice growled, anger and frustration practically radiating off him like waves of magic.

I swallowed and kept my gaze away from the victim. "Any witnesses?"

"One neighbour saw the victim return home in a cab about thirty minutes before the call came through. Another neighbour witnessed the fiancé come home around the same time. We're unsure about who returned home first, but no one else was observed entering or exiting the home. This happened quickly and violently. The fiancé is not on scene, but no one saw anyone leave. We had someone run out to get a chicken. It's in the bathroom you passed," Jacobs said, nodding toward the ensuite bathroom. "We've also called for a dog."

A tracking dog. The department usually only sent out one, again because of budget cuts, but it was a smart move. There was no way the person who did this got away without being covered with blood.

"Do you want me to raise her now or do you want to wait for the dog?" I asked.

"Do it now." Kang turned away and pulled his phone from his pocket. I hadn't even heard it ring.

"I can't talk right now," he grumbled into the phone.

I exchanged a look with Jacobs. His partner shrugged.

"How is this like the last scene?" I asked. "The

killer from that one was already found and he's dead. What are the chances this is just a coincidence?"

"Little to none," Kang growled as he stuffed his phone into his pocket. "Her stab wounds are consistent with the other victim's. We're hoping the spirit can answer those questions."

SIXTEEN

"Am I still pretty?" Tianna asked. "Am I still beautiful?"

A shiver spread up my spine as the latest victim echoed eerily familiar words. I shook off the feeling of dread and rolled my shoulders back. "Hello, Tianna. My name is Lark. I'm a necromancer and I raised you on behalf of the VicPD. I know this is a confusing time, but we need to know who or what did this to you."

The spirit stared at her mangled body, sadness pulling down her expression. She had been brutally stabbed repeatedly in the chest and stomach area. And like Addison, she also had a concentration of wounds around her upper thighs, suggesting her killer had tried to hack off her legs, too. "I...I don't believe it."

"Who did this to you, Tianna?"

"I had so much more I wanted to do."

"Tianna, I need a name. Help us catch the person responsible."

The victim pulled her attention away from the brutal scene and focused on me. "My fiancé."

"I need you to confirm his name."

"Jimmy Stewart."

I whispered over my shoulder to the detectives. "The victim has identified Jimmy Stewart as the murderer."

"The fiancé." Jacobs grunted and left the room while Kang remained stoically beside me.

"Why did your fiancé do this?" I asked,

Tianna shook her head. "Jimmy was so mad. So angry." She sniffed. "I couldn't reason with him. I couldn't...I couldn't stop him. He just kept stabbing me."

I nodded. "Do you know what made him so angry? Can you explain the sequence of events that led to this?"

Tianna vibrated. She folded her phantom arms over her chest and shook. "It's my fault. This is all my fault."

"This is not your fault, Tianna. No matter what you did or think you did, you didn't deserve this. No one does."

Tianna bit her lip, her gaze sliding to her corpse again. I wouldn't be able to hold her much longer without applying more force.

"Maybe I didn't deserve it, but I caused this," she whispered.

"How?" I asked. "What did you do? What happened?"

Tianna shook her head. Her long phantom hair brushing over her face. "It doesn't matter now. Please put me back."

The spirit tugged on my control.

"Let me go," Tianna said, more forceful now. "I don't want to be here anymore. I don't want these feelings. Send me back to the void, to the veil. I didn't feel anything there."

The tugging became a yank. I could hold her, of course. I had enough power. Forcing a soul to stay gave me the ick, though, and eventually, I'd need more blood.

Forcing her wouldn't be necessary. I still had access to Tianna's bones, which meant I could call her back at any time if the police needed more information.

"I release you, Tianna," I said, keeping my voice low and calm. "You can rest now."

Tianna's spirit stopped shaking and she took an audible breath in and out, even though the spirit had no need for breathing at all.

Gripping my magic, I sent Tianna's spirit across the veil. Hopefully, the victim could find some peace.

"We could've gotten more from her," Kang grumbled.

"Maybe, but I refuse to abuse or harass a spirit.

They deserve rest." I turned to find Kang studying me like one might a specimen at the zoo. "She might be more helpful after her soul has settled into the veil a bit. This was a traumatic death. Her essence needs time to accept its new reality."

He nodded and cleared his throat. "So she thinks this was her fault?"

"Don't a lot of victims of domestic abuse feel that way?"

Kang's stern expression crumpled for a brief second. In that moment, I caught a glimpse at just how much this crime scene affected him.

"Kang." I reached forward.

He pulled away and turned toward the hallway. A second later, Jacobs walked into the room, gaze flicking between the two of us. "The dog is here."

PLASTIC BOOTIES ABANDONED, I walked with Kang behind the tracker. Jacobs had tucked another chicken under his arm, cradling it to the side of his body like a rugby ball, "just in case."

The Belgian Malinois had taken one sniff of a shirt and went to work. The path was clear.

As if possessing an uncanny sense himself, Jacobs

already stood by the back gate, ready to open it when the police dog charged in that direction.

We headed toward the woods that bordered the suburban development and ran along a river.

Jacobs dropped back to walk alongside us, exchanging a look with Kang.

I didn't need to ask them to know what they were thinking because I had the same thoughts. This case was eerily similar to the last one I consulted on, just as Kang said. And that meant this dog chase would end with another gruesome scene.

"How did you know?" I asked them. "How did you know this murder was connected with the last one before I raised Tianna?"

Kang shrugged. "Gut feeling."

"And the wounds on the body," Jacobs added.

We made our way down a dusty dirt trail, our boots crushing sunbaked pine needles. I held my breath the entire time, dreadful anticipation twisting my stomach and squeezing my lungs.

Shouts from ahead carried down the trail to us. A few barks. The dog whined.

They'd found the fiancé, and given the lack of orders being shouted, the fiancé wasn't resisting arrest.

We entered a clearing and the other officers moved to let us through.

Jacobs grunted.

Kang swore.

One of the cops lurched to the side of the clearing and puked on the salal bush.

The fiancé lay in a desiccated heap on the forest floor with an almost identical serene expression—his phone in one hand and a bloody knife in the other. As with Darren, he looked like someone had vacuum-packed his body, and both his wrists had been slit.

I had glimpsed pictures of the couple earlier. Their apartment was full of photos. Jimmy hadn't been gaunt. Not like this.

He'd been a healthy man in his prime and some-thing made him snap, kill his fiancé and then somehow, end up here, drained of all his bodily fluids.

"How much do you want to bet there's a suicide note on that phone?" I asked.

Jacobs grunted.

Kang turned away from the scene and met my gaze. "We have a serial killer."

I nodded and swallowed. My palms grew clammy.

"Is demon possession a thing?" Jacobs leaned over and asked.

"How would I know?"

He blinked at me. "You're a necromancer."

"I've never encountered a demon, nor someone possessed by a demon. At least not that I know of. I deal with souls in the veil, the space that surrounds the ethereal plane of mortality. Necromancy theory claims demons exist, but they're beyond the veil, beyond our reach. A witch, on the other hand, might be able to reach through or past the veil, but that's beyond my scope of abilities or understanding."

Jacobs nodded.

Silence settled over the three of us and the detectives both stared at me and waited. Right. It was my time to shine. And sometimes, like right now, I hated my job.

I turned to Jacobs and held my hands out. He wordlessly handed over the chicken.

"Buckle up, boys." I stepped toward the body. "Let's see what Jimmy has to say."

CHAPTER SEVENTEEN

I sat in the passenger seat of Kang's gray sedan. If someone asked me what kind of car he drove, I'd say gray. It was an electric car with a clean interior, black leather seats and a large touch screen. He drove a nice car that smelled new. I'm not sure what I expected—a dusty station wagon with an interior smelling of cheesies, coffee and long stakeouts, maybe? I should've known better. Of course, Kang would maintain a clinically clean vehicle. Clinical and unfeeling, like his personality. His house probably had bare walls, or artwork strategically placed by an interior decorator.

We travelled through town in silence, both of us lost to our own thoughts as Kang drove. I tried really hard not to recall the details from the crime scenes and failed.

Jacobs had stayed at the second scene until the

shift change and Kang offered to drive me home. I might find the detective abrasive, but at least I didn't have to worry about maintaining an awkward conversation with a cab driver.

Turned out, Jimmy didn't have much to say at all. His confusion and anger after I raised him reminiscent of Darren's. He confessed to killing Tianna in an inexplicable fit of rage, trying to hack her body into pieces to dispose of her body, and getting consumed with disgust and grief before killing himself.

Kang was right. They had a serial killer. And they had to be a glamy. Was a vampire mind controlling the men and then somehow sucking them dry without leaving a mark after they made the men kill their partners? But why? What was the motive? Sheer evil didn't exist in isolation. There was always a cause, always a trigger.

Was this the work of a necromancer using spirits to enact violence? Normally, I sensed death magic in use, but the crime scenes didn't have anything like that. So if a necromancer was involved, the magic had to be cast somewhere else. What about witches or demons or both? Did these deaths serve to propel the culprit toward their endgame somehow or were these random acts of violence purely chaos or feeding a sadistic pleasure?

"Do you think there's a point to all of it?" Kang asked out of the blue.

If the same thought hadn't just bounced around my

own head, I might've been confused, but I wasn't. Apparently, we thought alike and that in itself disturbed me. "I don't know. Is there anything that connects the victims aside from their CODs, genders, and order of deaths?"

He tightened his grip on the steering wheel. "Nothing we've found so far."

I pressed my head back into the headrest and closed my eyes. "Do you think the perpetrator is trying to make a statement?"

"Oh, they've definitely made one," Kang said. "But usually murderers that are trying to make a political or societal point leave obvious calling cards or messages."

"This had nothing."

"No," he agreed. "I don't know how to explain it, but the murders felt very personal." He tapped his finger on the wheel. "The men's bodies don't look like a vamp kill, but we can't rule out the possibility."

"Gregor said it wasn't him or his men." The words came out before I could rethink them, and I winced. I hadn't meant to share that information, but maybe it was best that Kang knew.

The detective stiffened. "Gregor? As in the Master Vampire of Victoria?"

"That's him." I tried to keep my tone chipper and failed miserably.

Silence stretched for the next two lights until Kang spoke again in a low voice. "Is that who you're dating now?"

"What?" I jerked back. "No."

He pressed his lips together.

Who I dated wasn't any of his business anyway, not unless they were criminals and jeopardized my ability to complete my job without bias, but maybe I should've let Kang think I dated a vampire. That would help avoid other, more uncomfortable questions.

"How do you know the Master Vampire of Victoria?"

Yup. Questions like that one. That was a question I couldn't answer. Not with Kang. At the end of the day, he was a police officer who upheld the laws and unsanctioned raisings, even those of the undead, were against the law. I could lose my license, and depending on the infraction, I could get charged.

"He knew my grandfather," I said.

"Really?" His eyebrows shot up.

Huh. I'd managed to shock him. "Yeah."

"And he came by to say hi out of the goodness of his heart?" Kang tightened his grip on the steering wheel.

"No, of course not. I wanted to know if he knew anything about my father's disappearance." There. Not quite a lie, but I'd definitely stretched the truth.

Technically, everything I said was true. That was the most important part about lying—keeping as close to the truth as possible. Not that I made a habit of telling lies.

Kang grew silent again. He already knew about my

missing father. The information was in the system, right there for him to read at his leisure.

"I'm sorry you haven't found any answers about your father," Kang said after the silence had stretched for two city blocks. "I'm also sorry you don't trust me enough to tell me the truth."

"Excuse me?"

"You have a tell when you lie," he said.

"I do not."

He nodded, the corner of his lips tugging up a little. "You do."

I folded my arms over my chest. "What is it then?"

He shook his head and clicked his tongue at me. "If I tell you, you'll try to hide it and I'll have to figure out whatever new tell you develop. I like knowing this one."

I groaned and flopped back in my seat.

"So?" he prodded.

Nope. I wasn't going to tell him my illegal secrets and get myself arrested.

I cringed.

Kang might not arrest me. He might even understand. He'd hurt a man who planned to kill me all those years ago, though we never spoke of it. So he might very well look the other way for me, like I did for him. But I didn't want to place him in a position where he had to make that choice. I might not like the guy, but I respected him.

"So?" I repeated Kang's question. "Are you going to

tell me when and how you started seeing and hearing spirits?"

The tug at his lips disappeared and his expression slipped into his cold, indifferent mask. "No."

"Then I guess we both get to keep our secrets tonight."

"I guess so."

EIGHTEEN

A soft breeze from the sea flowed over my face as I walked beside Hudson on the sidewalk that ran along the waterfront. We'd shared a nice dinner at a local downtown restaurant and Hudson suggested we take a stroll along the seaside walkway.

As much as the seawall was a tourist attraction, filled with swarms of people, and I most definitely was not a tourist, I loved this part of Victoria. It boasted beautiful views of the downtown harbour, the Empress and the parliament buildings.

Hudson slipped my hand in his, our palms pressing together.

I smiled and squeezed his hand in response. This was nice. This was...normal. It had been a long time since I did something as simple as hold a man's hand and walk around. Hudson still had an edge to him, though. A mystery. And part of his allure was my need to figure out his secrets.

"So tell me more about your work," I said. Most of our conversation had revolved around my job. Not a surprise, it was often the focus of conversation on the rare occasion I went out on dates. Unlike past men, though, Hudson appeared intrigued, not scared or disgusted.

He shrugged and looked toward the water. "Not much to tell. I purchase companies for clients, dismantle them, and then merge them to become more efficient and productive."

"You just don't seem like the corporate business type," I said. But why did that job sound hot?

His mouth twitched and he peered down at me. "Don't I?"

"Maybe I need to see you in a suit."

His gaze twinkled.

Or maybe I needed to see him out of one. "I'm not getting a ruthless vibe from you."

His smile widened and he leaned down. "I can be ruthless when I need to be."

"Is that so?"

"Mmmm." His blue gaze flashed in the moonlight. "It's all about knowing how to apply the right pressure."

"Are we still talking about your work?"

"It's not work if you're having fun." He winked.

We were definitely not talking about his work

anymore. The heat from the summer's day had already dissipated, but my body flushed with warmth.

"What about hobbies?" I blurted out. "Surely you have some downtime between destroying businesses?"

"Aside from working out, reading, sleeping, keeping the house tidy and myself fed?"

I widened my eyes dramatically. "Your muscles aren't natural? I'm so disappointed."

He laughed. "I also like to collect antique relics."

I raised my eyebrows. That was unexpected, even more so than his day job. "What kind of antiques?"

He paused and glanced down at me again, almost as if to check my sincerity. Had previous dates mocked him when they learned this information? "Books, mostly. I like maps and paintings as well."

"What got you into that?" I asked.

"Family. My parents were collectors as well."

"So you don't believe in keeping the past in the past?"

"I think the past has the power to guide our future, but not in a bad way, at least not necessarily. We remember our past so we can learn from it and avoid making the same mistakes."

I peered up at him, taking in his serene expression. "Maybe you should've been a guidance counsellor."

He laughed again. He had a lovely laugh, one that was warm and welcoming and made me want to laugh along, even if I didn't know the joke. "Not as much pay in that."

My phone buzzed, but I ignored it. Hudson's gaze captivated me, and we'd stopped walking. Standing in the middle of the seawall walkway, we leaned into each other, ignoring the tourists milling around nearby. Hudson's gaze dropped to my lips.

My phone buzzed again.

Hudson pulled back. "Are you going to get that?"

I mentally cursed the caller. "Nope."

Would it come across desperate if I reached up and tried to pull him back toward me? I wanted to feel his lips pressed to mine. We hadn't kissed yet, but the chemistry zinging between us gave me hope it would be electric. But the stupid device in my purse vibrated again. It didn't change—same tone and vibration, but it just seemed louder and angrier.

"Are you sure about that?" Hudson asked. Despite being a ruthless businessman, he hadn't checked his phone once during our date—something I greatly appreciated.

I sighed and stepped away to dig the phone out of my purse.

Of course, it was Kang.

I held up my finger to ask Hudson to give me a minute and swore under my breath.

He nodded and I tapped the screen.

"What?" I hissed.

"We have a lead." Kang's deep voice vibrated the phone.

"Good for you," I said. "Did you need me for something or did you want a personal cheering squad?"

Kang grew quiet and I envisioned him gnashing his teeth together. "Oh, I'm sorry. Am I interrupting another date?"

"It's my night off, Kang."

"Must be nice. I haven't had one of those in a decade."

I smiled, imagining Kang in a Hawaiian T-shirt with his feet up on some beach. He'd be in paradise and probably still scowl and snap at everyone.

"A night off or a date?" I asked.

Kang growled into the phone. "Call me when you're back to work. We need your help." He hung up before I had a chance to say anything wittier or even maybe just mutter a goodbye. I glanced at my phone before throwing it back in my purse.

Hudson watched me the entire time, his gaze missing the heat from a few moments ago. Kang's phone call had effectively ruined our moment.

Jerk. He didn't even have to be nearby to ruin my night.

"Come on," Hudson said. "Let's head back."

CHAPTER NINETEEN

I threw my keys on the counter and glared at the clock. Hudson had dropped me off and kissed me on the cheek after walking me to the front door. He was the perfect example of a gentleman.

He'd probably ghost me now.

I may as well accept it instead of getting my hopes up for a third date. Normally, men disappeared after they found out what I did for work. They didn't stick around long enough to get annoyed with my work schedule.

Ten at night and nowhere to go. I called Kang back.

He picked up on the third ring. "I thought you were on a date."

"Well, I was, but a call from the cops tends to put a damper on things."

Kang chuckled. "You didn't have to pick up."

"Really? You calling three times in a row suggested otherwise."

"Things couldn't have been that hot if a phone call—"

"Three phone calls."

"...if three phone calls put the fire out."

I ground my teeth together and squeezed the phone. Plastic creaked.

"Better that he knows your schedule now, Morgan, than find out later," Kang said, his tone softening. He almost sounded like he cared. "Not a lot of people can handle our workload and it's better if those that can't, cut and run before you get emotionally invested."

I glanced at the phone screen. Yup. I'd called Kang, not my therapist. "Look at you, dishing out life advice."

"Trying to butter you up."

I narrowed my eyes, even though Kang couldn't see me. "Why?"

"We found a link between the two victims."

"You have me aflutter with anticipation."

Kang grunted. I could just picture him staring at his phone and debating whether to hang up on me. "Both women were at the same club on the night of their murders. Credit card receipts show them withdrawing money from the same machine."

"Okay..." Seriously, I liked a good murder-mystery as much as the next person, but Kang didn't make a habit of sharing this kind of information, and I failed to see how this new information involved me.

When I'd first started working as a consultant for the police, I'd wanted to be involved, begged even. I'd wanted to know all the details to help with the investigation. It had been Kang—Mr. fucking sunshine himself—who'd quickly disavowed me of that notion. He told me, very bluntly, to leave the detecting to the detectives and they'd leave the death raising to the death raiser.

I scowled at the memory.

"I'd like you to go to the club with me," Kang said.

"Say what?"

He didn't repeat himself, he let the silence speak for him.

"What do you expect me to do? Find bones in the basement and command a legion of lost souls to solve the case?"

"Can you actually do that?"

"No."

"Too bad."

"Kang."

"Morgan."

I took a deep breath and tried to speak as calmly as possible. "I distinctly recall you telling me, not so kindly, I might add, that I wasn't a detective. Last I checked, my status hasn't changed."

"Well, we need it to change for this case," he replied, huffy. "Just for a little bit."

"Why? You have female officers who can do undercover."

"Maybe I want you to go with me."

Now that couldn't be right. I waited.

Kang sighed. "We know this is glamy related. We thought it would be handy to have you along in case it involves something from the veil and you can sense it."

"So you want to bring me along as a glamy detection system?"

"Pretty much."

Maybe I should be offended, but I wasn't. I already knew I'd say yes. So did Kang. Any chance to go on an investigation, I'd take it. But yanking Kang's chain just made everything more enjoyable.

"Where are we going?"

"A club called Spiral."

CHAPTER

TWENTY

Detectives Kang and Jacobs met me outside the club. Spiral had been around for years, but after new owners purchased it, and a famous influencer subsequently raved about it, the club became the newest hotspot in Victoria. Unfortunately, this wasn't an undercover operation, so I didn't get to show up in my best clubbing attire and adopt a stage name. Instead, I'd resigned myself to wearing my leather pants and vest that also doubled as my work clothes. I didn't know where the night would take us so I may as well be prepared.

As a compromise, I wore heels.

Kang and Jacobs turned at my approach. Jacobs flashed me his ever-ready smile. He'd gelled his hair a little and wore nicely cut jeans and a white collared shirt with the top button undone. He looked like the

188

good guy ready to cut loose and the women inside the club would eat it up.

Like day and night, Kang was his polar opposite. Dark and brooding, he couldn't say "dangerous" more clearly if he had a neon sign flashing over his head. He wore dark-washed jeans, and a black collared shirt that matched his hair, the stubble on his jaw, and undoubtedly, his soul.

"Did you two coordinate? I'm a little hurt not to be included in the memo." I flicked my finger between the two.

Kang scowled and that only made Jacobs' grin widen. "Not on purpose. But I should've known." Jacobs hitched his thumb in Kang's direction. "He's the dark and broody type."

Hah! Those were the same words I used to describe Kang all the time. I closed the distance between them and batted my eyelashes at Jacobs. "And what type are you?"

"The annoying type," Kang answered for his partner. "Let's go inside."

We approached the bouncer. Kang leaned in to speak quietly in the large man's ear.

The bouncer glowered at the detective. His lips moved, but I couldn't make out what he said.

Both Jacobs and Kang reached for their back pockets to pull out their wallets and flash their identification.

The bouncer looked ready to argue but must've

thought better of it and stepped to the side instead. He reached for the ear opposite of Kang and said something into the radio, probably letting the manager know.

When I moved to follow the detectives, the bouncer shook his head.

"She's with us," Kang growled.

"Lucky bitch." A woman with beautiful red hair and naturally pouty lips complained at the front of the line.

I winked at her before stepping into the club. Warm air, heavy bass and a thick waft of cologne and booze hit my face.

A man in a gray suit, minus the jacket, waited for us near the entrance. He had a chunky gold ring on his pinky finger and a shiny watch that probably cost more than what three of my paycheques would cover. He was most likely in his late thirties and the shirt fit him so well, it revealed a fit, lean torso. He had black hair, tanned skin, gray eyes and one of those smiles that seemed entirely too white. If I wasn't seeing him in person, I'd assume he used some sort of tooth whitening filter.

"Grant Malone." He stepped forward and offered his hand for Kang to shake.

We took turns introducing ourselves and shaking his hand with me being last. His touch made my skin tingle, but he wasn't a necromancer, and he certainly wasn't dead.

"Lark?" He cocked his head. "An interesting name. Not one you hear often."

I shrugged, unsure of how to reply. The girls from school had made fun of my name growing up, too, but thankfully, I'd moved past being insecure about what made me different. For the most part, at least.

"I'm one of the owners of the club," Grant said. "The bouncer radioed up and said this was about an active investigation. How can I help the VicPD?"

"We would like to view your security footage."

Grant raised his eyebrows. "Do you have a warrant?"

"Not yet. But we can get one," Kang said. "We're not concerned about the club's activities."

"Then what are you concerned about?" Grant folded his arms in front of his chest. The fabric of his shirt pulled up to show off his toned arm muscles.

Kang shot me an annoyed glance.

What? Had I made a sound? I couldn't help noticing an attractive man with a fit body.

"A murderer," Kang replied.

He was so dramatic.

Grant widened his eyes, and he glanced between the two serious detectives before his gaze settled on me again. "And what's your part in this?"

Mighty fine question. I wasn't sure how to answer. Should I tell him I tagged along in case I could sense evil spirits? That would go over so well.

"Supervising," I said.

Jacobs snorted and then tried to hide his laughter with fake coughing.

Kang squinted at me, his mouth turned down. "Ms. Morgan is here as a consultant."

Grant scanned my body, up and down, and his expression turned appreciative. His gaze, though... Maybe it was the strobe lights, or the angle, but those eyes appeared harder, calculating.

"May we please view the video feeds?" Jacobs asked. "Evidence traces two victims back to this location on the same night of their deaths."

"I'll make you a deal." Grant kept his gaze on me.

Kang stiffened.

"You let me take Lark out on the dance floor and you can view all the security footage you want."

"Absolutely not," Kang answered immediately.

Grant shrugged. "Then go get your warrant. I'm sure some judge will appreciate the Saturday night phone call."

"Kang." I reached out to touch his arm.

He jerked away. "No, Lark."

Kang calling me by my first name did weird things to my insides and I did not want to pause to think too hard about why.

"It's just a dance," I said. It was a dick move on Grant's part, but one dance wouldn't hurt me, and it would be a lot faster than waiting on a warrant.

"You're not chattel to be bartered." Kang leaned down and hissed in my ear.

"You're absolutely right." I stepped close, purposefully placing myself between Kang and Grant. "And I'm also my own person. While I appreciate you looking out for me, you don't get to make decisions for me. I'm going to dance with this guy, and you better make my sacrifice worth it."

Kang pressed his lips together. His hands curled into fists.

"You can stay down here and guard me. Send Jacobs up."

"Fine." He jerked his chin in Jacobs' direction.

His partner rolled his eyes and walked away, presumably to find the office.

I turned to find Grant wearing a smug smile. He held his hand out and I took it, letting him lead me to the dance floor while I concocted my plan.

Kang was right.

I wasn't chattel and Grant had the audacity to try to barter with Kang over me instead of directing his negotiations my way.

Fine. It was all *fine*.

I'd make him regret his decision and hopefully, Kang enjoyed the show.

CHAPTER
TWENTY-ONE

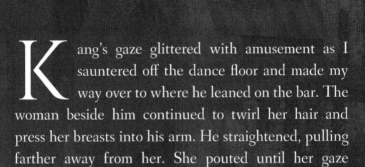

Kang's gaze glittered with amusement as I sauntered off the dance floor and made my way over to where he leaned on the bar. The woman beside him continued to twirl her hair and press her breasts into his arm. He straightened, pulling farther away from her. She pouted until her gaze flicked over to me. With a sigh, she plucked her drink from the bar and walked away from Kang.

"Making friends?" I nodded at the retreating woman.

"Not if I can help it." Kang held out a glass of water. "You're a phenomenally bad dancer." He nodded over my shoulder, and I turned in time to watch Grant limp off the dance floor toward his office.

I took a long sip of the cold water before responding. "Maybe. Or maybe I just need the right partner."

Kang dipped his head back and laughed. "You danced that poorly on purpose? Now that's talent."

"I have many talents, Kang. You just haven't noticed them."

He lifted his own glass of water from the counter and took a sip. "Oh, I noticed."

I narrowed my eyes. Was he joking or serious? It was always so hard to tell with him.

Kang frowned and pulled his phone from his pocket. It must've been on silent because I didn't hear it ring. Then again, with the music cranked this loud, I could barely hear Kang speaking.

Kang scowled at the screen before sliding the phone back into his pocket.

"Who was that?"

"No one."

I folded my arms in front of my chest. "It was definitely someone."

"Let me amend my original statement. No one important."

Ouch. That poor woman. And it would've been a woman. I'd known Kang long enough to identify him for the serial, non-committal, monogamist that he was. His current girlfriend—or whatever he referred to her as—probably wanted to be something or someone to Kang, but Kang preferred to stay unattached.

"Right," I said. "Because you're the 'love them and leave them' type of guy."

"First of all, love isn't involved with any of the

women I date, and I always make that very clear from the start. Second of all, you seem pretty fired up for someone who hates being in my presence, and third of all...maybe I'm like you with your dancing. I just need to find the right partner."

Before I could respond, a familiar voice cut through the constantly booming background of the club. "Lark?"

I turned to find Hudson standing a few feet away. He still wore the same clothes from our date.

What the hell?

Had he dropped me off to drive here and find a replacement?

"What are you doing here?" he asked.

Funny. I wondered the same thing. "I'm here on a case. Hudson, this is Detective Kang. Kang this is Hudson." I purposefully left out Hudson's last name. I wouldn't put it past Kang to run a background check on my date just to tease me with the information. He'd done it before.

Hudson turned to Kang, and they exchanged brief greetings and a quick handshake.

"And you?" I asked. "What brings you to Spiral?"

"Grant is a client. I helped him and his business partner secure this establishment along with a few others. I was restless and decided to come over and finish up some paperwork."

Kang took a long sip of water, suspiciously long. Like he was trying to keep his mouth busy to prevent himself from talking. But I knew what he'd say, and it wasn't anything I wasn't already thinking. I appreciated the effort, though. I didn't need his smartass comments right now.

Disappointment tugged at my gut and squeezed my chest. And like Kang, I remained quiet. I'd only been on two dates with Hudson. We weren't sleeping together. We weren't exclusive. He didn't owe me anything. I'd also been restless and that's how I ended up here, stomping on the owner's toes. I had no place or position in Hudson's life to be upset, yet I was.

"Didn't really peg this place as your scene," I said.

He scrunched his nose. "It's not."

Awkward silence fell over the three of us, despite the club's loud music.

"I'm done with the paperwork now. Why don't we finish our date? We could stay here or there's a coffee shop always open late. It's just across the street."

"Our date already ended," I pointed out.

"Not the way I wanted it to."

Oh.

"Right," Kang interjected before I could respond. "I'll go help Jacobs with the footage. Thank you for your help tonight, Morgan. We'll call if we require any further services."

Any further services?

Um.

"Hey, Kang?" I called out.

He hesitated before turning enough to glance at me over his shoulder.

"I don't hate it." He'd implied I didn't like being in his presence, and as accurate as that might've been a few years ago, the guy was kind of growing on me. And for some reason, I needed to tell him. I couldn't let him leave and think he was right when he made that comment.

He jerked his chin up and down in a brief nod and stalked off toward the office.

That made no sense. Why was he leaving exactly? Kang had brought me here to sense bad spirits, not barter for access to security footage. Why would he just leave me here now? He should be relishing in the awkwardness of this moment, not running away from it.

"What was that about?" Hudson asked.

"Just work politics," I lied, but I had no truthful answer to give.

TWENTY-TWO

I flung myself in my work chair and dropped my head back on the leather cushion. The lights at Raisers made a humming sound and I closed my eyes and let the familiarity of my surroundings comfort me.

After Kang left me in the club with Hudson, I'd lasted ten minutes of more awkward small talk before making an excuse to go home. That was two nights ago. I hadn't heard from Kang or Hudson since, and instead, I filled my evenings raising the dead the good old-fashioned, legal way.

My body ached and tingled as if I'd ran some sort of race or spent the evening hiking instead of death raising. I'd sleep well tonight.

The red flashing light on my office phone said I might have to wait.

With a deep sigh, I picked up the receiver and pressed the button to access my voicemail.

"Morgan, it's Kang. Call me." His deep voice vibrated the receiver while his words confused me. Why had he called my work phone? Were we back to that now? Already? He had my cell number.

I pulled out my phone, found Kang's contact information and tapped the call icon.

He picked up on the second ring. "About fucking time, Morgan."

"Just got into my office, jerk. Why did you call my work phone? If you needed me urgently, you have my cell number."

"Jerk? Seriously?"

"Yes, seriously. You're always swearing at me. Why didn't you call my cell?"

He paused. Silence filled the time long enough for me to check my phone to see if he'd hung up on me.

"I was trying to be respectful of your space," he finally growled.

"What does that even mean?"

"He didn't want to interrupt any more of your dates," Jacobs yelled somewhere in the background. "Said you needed all the help you could get."

I rolled my eyes even though neither of them could see me. "You're ridiculous."

"Me or him?" Kang asked.

"Both."

"Harsh," he said.

Jacobs laughed maniacally in the background.

"So..." I prompted.

"So, we have a couple of updates on our cases we thought you'd be interested in. First, the preliminary autopsy report came back from the first set of deaths. Darren's body was decomposed. The coroner placed his death at a time inconsistent with the death of Addison."

"But he was covered with her blood and so was the knife. And he had defensive wounds. That doesn't make sense."

"Not if we're excluding glamies."

"Do you know any glamy capable of doing that?" I asked.

"Not yet."

I blew out a breath. He had a point. Just because we weren't aware of something didn't mean it didn't exist. "So what does this mean?"

"It means Addison and Darren Riley's deaths are not going to be officially ruled as a murder-suicide and we keep investigating."

"So nothing has changed?" And I'm now left more confused than before.

"Not quite. We finished going over the video footage. It took some time, but we found our two victims."

I sat up in my chair.

"They both danced with men who were not their partners."

"That doesn't necessarily mean anything," I said. Though it did look bad.

"Morgan, there are three types of dancing," Kang said. "There's normal, having a good time dancing, there's whatever the fuck you did to that guy on the dance floor the other night, and then there's what these women were doing."

"That bad?"

"Pretty sure Jacobs needed a smoke afterward."

"I thought he quit."

"He did, but it was a close call. He almost relapsed."

Jacobs muttered something, but I missed it.

"Anyway," Kang continued. "One of the men paid for drinks using his credit card and the other plays for the local hockey team so we recognized him right away. Both are headed to the station tomorrow for questioning. Would you like to tag along for the interviews? See if you can pick up anything?"

I swallowed the squeal threatening to erupt from my soul, knowing that if one escaped my lips, Kang would rescind the offer. "I love it when you talk dirty to me."

Kang laughed and hung up.

JACOBS AND KANG led me through the main area of the precinct. Some of the officers stopped to wave or say hello, including Daniels and Rodriguez. I didn't come down here often, only making an appearance when my signature was needed, and I could sign a lot of forms digitally now. The place smelled of paper, metal and disinfectant, the walls barren with the exception of a few informational posters.

We passed the holding cells and I skidded to a stop. A familiar muscle-bound man looked up from where he sat. In the club, with the dark lighting, he'd appeared handsome, but the bright fluorescent lights revealed the roughness of his skin, receding hairline and thinning hair. His eyes stayed the same—the brilliant blue flashing with anger as he glared at me. He didn't look nearly so confident in the holding cell and part of me wanted to march in there and bruise his wrist to make things even.

The detectives both stopped and turned to me, an almost identical question in their gazes.

"I know that guy." I jabbed my finger in the air at Gym Bro. "He grabbed my wrist in a club."

"Oh really?" Kang shrugged and turned to walk away.

"Kang..." I didn't even know where to start. "I said I handled it."

He turned back and stepped in close. He bent his head to whisper into my ear, "The next time someone lays a finger on you, let *me* handle it."

203

Without waiting for a response, Kang stalked off toward the interrogation rooms.

Jacobs snorted and watched his partner leave before leaning in. "We had some complaints about this guy getting a little too hands-on at the clubs."

I swallowed and tried really hard not to look at my wrist.

"After he saw you all bruised up, Kang was determined to hunt him down and charge him with anything possible. Turns out, this guy is years overdue for child support and there's a warrant out in Alberta for him in connection to a domestic abuse allegation. The RCMP will be picking him up soon and transporting him to face charges."

My mouth fell open and I consciously had to close it before it caught some flies. "Well...that's good news."

"Isn't it?" Jacobs beamed at me and waved his arm for me to walk ahead of him.

Kang had hunted down the guy who hurt me? How did he even find him? I never mentioned the club's name nor did I give a description. Sure, he was a detective, but that was a lot of work to go through for a bruised wrist. Especially when I was fairly certain Kang wanted to throttle me himself.

A memory of the two detectives huddled together when I walked out of the washroom with a chicken flashed in my mind. They were probably already conspiring to find the guy back then.

Maybe I needed to evaluate why I thought Kang

despised me so much and why I was so determined to paint the detective as a bad guy when clearly he wasn't.

And maybe I needed to shove this personal shit to the side and focus on the case.

I waved a silent goodbye to Jacobs and stepped into the interrogation viewing room. I held my breath. I'd always wanted to see one of these in person instead of on the television in one of the true crime dramas I binged. The viewing room smelled like coffee, sweat and more metal. On the other side of the glass, Johnny Thompson, a handsome man wearing a floral-pattern shirt at least one size too small, sat on the opposite side of the table from Kang and an empty seat. A well-dressed lawyer with a gray suit, pinstriped tie and tired eyes had joined Johnny, sitting beside him.

Kang and Jacobs had told me the guy's name when I arrived. They planned to interrogate Johnny first and the professional hockey player second, and butterflies did flips in my belly from my barely contained excitement.

"Thank you for coming in, Johnny." Jacobs walked into the room and shut the door behind him. He took the empty seat beside Kang. Of course, he'd be the good cop. One look at Kang's grumpy-ass face and no one would doubt which role he'd play.

"Just to reiterate what we spoke about over the phone, you're not under arrest and your answers to our questions are voluntary," Jacobs continued. "You're also free to leave at any time. We've asked you here today because we need your help."

Johnny nodded and swallowed.

"Do you know this woman?" Kang slid a photo across the table.

I couldn't see around his shoulders, so I glanced up at the monitor that showed the overhead view of the table. Kang hadn't shown Johnny the crime scene photo. Instead, he'd selected one from Addison's social media that showed her beautiful smile and sleek hair.

Johnny paled. "I...I think so. I met her in a club."

Well, he wasn't lying yet, so that was a good sign.

"What was the nature of your relationship with Addison Riley?"

Johnny frowned and leaned in to whisper to his lawyer.

The lawyer, whose name I hadn't caught, received the information without changing his facial expression. After a pause, he turned to Johnny and nodded.

"I didn't have a relationship," Johnny said. "We met at a club. Had some drinks and fu...had sex in one of the stalls in the men's washroom."

My eyebrows shot up to my hairline, but Kang and Jacobs took in the information the same way the lawyer had. I couldn't see their faces, but their bodies remained relaxed, and I knew the two well enough to know they'd remain expressionless.

"What happened after the bathroom?" Kang asked.

Johnny shrugged. "She left and I kept partying with the boys."

"Where did you go after the club?" Jacobs asked.

"Home."

Kang leaned forward. "Can anyone verify that?"

"Sure." Johnny bobbed his head up and down. "My roommate, Pat, was the designated driver. Sober as a judge."

I bit my lip. I knew a few judges and they weren't exactly poster children for sobriety, at least not during their time off. They saw too much shit and some of them self-medicated.

Kang slid a pad of lined paper and a pen across the table to Johnny. "We'll need his contact information."

"Will we find your DNA on Addison?"

"I mean...maybe? We used protection, but...Wait. What do you mean on her? Is she okay? Did something happen?" He paled. "Did she accuse me of something?"

Jacobs leaned back in his seat. "Should she have?"

"No!" Johnny's eyes grew to twice their size. "It was her idea. She was very...enthusiastic."

Kang glanced at Jacobs, a silent message travelling between them, before turning back to Johnny. "Ms. Riley is dead. Someone killed her sometime after the club."

Johnny snapped his mouth shut and froze.

"We're trying to piece together the sequence of events that led up to her murder. Establish a timeline.

We'd appreciate it if you could think back to that evening and recall any additional details," Kang continued. "Did she say anything or do anything to indicate she feared for her safety? Was anyone following or harassing her?"

"No," Johnny whispered. "She was a fun-loving woman looking for some d..." He swallowed, his gaze shifted from left to right. "Action."

"If you think of anything, please get in touch." Jacobs placed his card beside the notepad. "In the meantime, please provide us with your roommate's contact information and the best way to get a hold of you. We may have more questions later. If you'd like to voluntarily submit your DNA, we'd appreciate that, too."

"My DNA?" Johnny stammered. "But you'll find it on her body."

"Yes," Jacobs said. "But from your own statement, we shouldn't find any at the crime scene or on the murder weapon. It will help us rule you out as a suspect."

Johnny glanced at his lawyer. Instead of speaking to his client, the lawyer stood and buttoned his suit jacket. "I think we're done here. I'll discuss the DNA with my client and get back to you."

"Of course." Jacobs stood and leaned over the table to shake their hands.

I leaned on the wall and folded my arms over my chest. The interview was a little anticlimactic compared to my expectations. Of course, I knew real life detective work was a lot less dramatic than the shows made them out to be, but I'd hoped Kang and Jacobs could get some helpful information from Johnny.

Instead, he'd just corroborated what Jacobs had gathered from the security footage and from the detectives' body language, Johnny hadn't given them any reason not to trust his word. They'd still follow up with the witnesses and DNA.

Kang walked into the viewing room after Johnny left. He studied me for a moment, a small smile tugging at his lips. "Everything you'd hoped for?"

The man knew my weaknesses.

"A bit of a letdown," I said instead. "Maybe I should bring some speakers next time and play some dramatic music to spice things up."

"You fucking loved it," he said.

I did. I enjoyed every second and he knew it. Detective work was my drug of choice and Kang held it in the palm of his hand.

THE SECOND INTERVIEW produced almost identical results to the first, except it had the added bonus of including a professional hockey player. I didn't even watch hockey anymore, but I'd resurrect that pastime for more glimpses of this beautiful man. Kang and Jacobs walked into the viewing room after they concluded the interview, and Kang held out a tissue.

"What's this for?" I plucked the tissue from his hand.

"The drool."

"We could hear you panting from the other room." Jacobs winked.

"You could not."

I used the tissue to dab my lips and chin, just in case.

Kang snorted.

I balled up the tissue and tossed it in the garbage before turning back to the detectives. "So both the victims cheated on their partners at the same club and ended up dead."

"Pretty much." Jacobs shoved his hands in his pockets. "The only difference is Mr. Professional Hockey player got in a fight with a random guy afterward outside a coffee shop."

"What's your next move?" I asked.

"I'm going to head back to the club tonight, and I also plan to check out the café to see if there's any video surveillance that caught the altercation." Kang pointed in my direction. "And you're coming with me."

"I am?"

"You are." Kang actually smiled. The effect was

devastating. "Jacobs has plans tonight and I need back up."

I turned to Jacobs. "Hot date?"

He grimaced. "Something like that."

Something wasn't adding up about all of this. I frowned. "We're in a building full of backup, Kang."

"True, but none of them can detect and deter glamy magic."

He had a point there. Thing was, I couldn't detect and deter all glamy magic, either. But the dead? I could conquer the dead.

CHAPTER

TWENTY-THREE

eat washed over me, filled with heavy
smells of sweat, cologne and booze. Heavy
bass thumped and rattled the walls. Young
and not-so-young patrons rubbed against each
other to the beat of the music.

"I'm too old for this shit," Kang said.

"You don't look a day over forty-five." I bit my
tongue and tried to keep my face relaxed.

Kang glowered. "Funny."

I shrugged. "You feel old, and I feel woefully
underdressed."

Kang dropped his gaze to my body before quickly
snapping his attention back to my face. He scanned the
crowd next, his lips pursed. "If anything, I'd say you
were overdressed."

"Wearing an obscene amount of leather." I crossed

my arms over my chest and did my best Kang impression.

He smirked. "Is that supposed to be me?"

"How'd I do?"

He shook his head. "Not even close."

"Can't win them all."

A bouncer with arm muscles bigger than my face approached us and leaned in to speak to Kang. The detective nodded and the man walked off. "What did he say?"

"Grant's not available at the moment."

"Convenient. Probably scared to talk to the cops again."

Kang flashed his teeth at me. "Honestly? I think you probably scare him more than I do."

If my dance with the manager had to be described by any onlooker, they'd probably call it physical assault *with flare*. "I regret nothing."

"Good." He scanned the room of gyrating people again, frowning.

"So what now?"

He shrugged. "I didn't really need to speak with Grant again, aside from asking some basic follow up questions to confirm the timeline."

"Then what are we doing here?"

He pointed at me.

"You'll have to be more specific."

"If there's something glamy going on, we can unravel this case."

"So just hang out until I sense something? You seem pretty confident I can moonlight as a glamy-detection alarm. You do realize my skills revolve around death, right? Unless it's a vampire, spirit or fellow necromancer we're hooped."

"You have many talents, Morgan. You said so yourself. I know you can do this."

I shook my head. If we were at the stage where I had to get motivational speeches from Kang, we were in deep shit. I may as well go home, have a bubble bath and drink some wine. I gave Kang a skeptical look. "Yes, but what makes you so sure I'm the person to help you?"

"If you dance with me, I'll tell you." He raised his eyebrows in a challenge.

"Are you insane?" I gaped at him. "You saw me dance. Why would you willingly subject yourself to that torture?"

"Maybe I'm hoping you'll deem me worthy of an actual dance instead of a sparring partner."

"We've been verbally battling for years, Kang. Are you sure you want to test my benevolence?" I narrowed my eyes. What was he getting at? He wasn't the dancing type. At least I didn't think he was. I didn't know much about Kang outside the professional arena, but he'd just proclaimed he was too old for this shit.

"Maybe." Kang leaned in. "And maybe I want us to blend in a bit instead of looking like judgemental parents standing off to the side."

A laugh escaped my lips, and I slapped my hand in his. "Okay."

His palm was surprisingly warm. Not hot and sweaty warm, just...nice. Solid. Calloused. Comforting in a way. He held my hand and led me onto the dance floor.

The club didn't favour fast beats or the kind of music I'd jump around to and wave my arms. Nope. Not my luck. This club played music with heavy bass.

Perfect for grinding.

Before I had a chance to process what this meant, Kang had me in his arms moving to the beat. He pulled me into the heat of his body, his hard chest flush with mine, his abs pressed to my torso, our hips aligned. He had one hand placed at the small of my back to keep me in place, while he wrapped the other around the back of my neck. It was possessive, and something dormant inside me stirred.

Instead of feeling trapped as I very well should, I felt the opposite—safe, and secure.

And very hot.

It got incredibly warm, incredibly quickly.

Kang could move and he was doing all sorts of things with his hips. Swaying and swivelling, he rocked me back and forth. The spark he'd ignited inside burst into full flames and heat spread through my body.

I was on fire.

At first, I just kind of stood there, letting him move

me around like a rag doll, too surprised to react, let alone dance.

"Come on, Morgan," Kang's voice rumbled along my skin. "We're trying to blend in. Move with me."

So I did.

Shamelessly. Dancing was such an odd thing. I was an average dancer at best. Sometimes when I danced with someone, it was like our timing was off. We'd bump into each other and move off beat...it just wasn't good or enjoyable because of the lack of chemistry.

That wasn't an issue with Kang. Maybe he was so skilled at dancing that he could make anything, anyone, work.

Or maybe we had chemistry.

What a horrendous thought.

We moved perfectly in sync with each other. Flaw-less. Like we were made to dance together. Kang watched me intently. When the song ended, fusing with the next, he didn't stop. Kang wasn't the type to falter or yield.

As if being in his arms offered a silent challenge to him, he kept moving me along to the music without missing a beat, a dark promise flashing in his gaze.

It didn't take much to imagine what this would feel like if we were naked. Kang would make love like this, with his entire focus on moving with me to make me feel like a fucking goddess.

Dear god, I probably wouldn't survive the experience.

The song ended and then the next. And the next. Kang finally did slow down, moving us to the edge of the dance floor. My heart raced. I probably panted like an overheating dog. I was one hip swivel away from dragging Kang into the washroom to find out if his mouth moved as well as his hips. I didn't dare look away from the intensity in his gaze.

"Did you know each spirit has its own unique smell?" he said.

What? I shook my head. That was the last thing I expected to come out of his mouth. He still held me in his arms and looked ready to devour me.

Here I was, imagining all sorts of lewd and indecent acts and his mind was still on the case.

Yeah, that wasn't embarrassing.

"Morgan?"

I took a deep breath and focused on his comment. "Yes. Actually. Spirit scents came up in one of my glamy courses when I went to university."

"You asked me how I'd be sure you could help. I know a spirit is involved with the murders. Its unique scent was at both crime scenes. I didn't realize it at the first set of murders. There were so many common scents on both Addison and Darren and detecting a random spirit at a scene isn't uncommon. It wasn't until the second set of crime scenes that I put it together. A spirit is definitely involved in the murders, whether it's actually causing them remains to be seen."

I had so many questions. So many. Which one did I start with? "How?"

My voice came out as a croak, so I swallowed and tried again. "How can you smell spirits? Only certain glamies can..."

Kang watched me, gaze intent, hyper-fixated on my face.

As far as I knew, Kang was human. He'd never claimed to be anything else, but then, that didn't mean he wasn't. The police only hired drabs as officers. Glamies like myself were good enough to use as consultants, but not good enough to trust or hire on a permanent basis with benefits and a pension.

If Kang was a glamy, he was hiding it from the force.

And he'd trusted me with the information.

"Who else knows?" I asked. Only a few types of glamy could sniff test a spirit. Which type was Kang? Would he be offended if I asked?

"Just Jacobs," he said.

I nodded. Made sense. Those two were close and Jacobs had always presented himself as a trustworthy comrade.

"You said my necromancy was only one of the reasons you wanted me here. What was the other?"

"I need to know something first," he said.

"Okay, sure."

"How serious is this thing you have going on with that guy?"

"What guy?"

"The one you ran into at this club the other night."

"Hudson? We've only gone on two dates." My heart pounded. There could be only one reason why he'd want to know. "Not serious at all."

He smiled then, a wide, genuine smile, the kind he didn't often use. His arms tightened around me, and he leaned down.

Before he had a chance to say anything, a wave of negative energy rolled over me. I stiffened in his arms and pushed away.

His expression shuttered and he straightened. "I see."

"No. Shhh." I pushed my magic out to probe the area. "Do you smell it? I sensed something."

"I smell your arousal and that thing you're sensing is my raging hard-on."

I swatted his arm. "Focus. I sensed a spirit. An angry one."

Kang frowned and looked around. Would he sniff the air?

I snorted and closed my eyes. The feeling of death lingered in the air a little, but no more negative vibes pinged my senses. I relaxed and opened my eyes. "False alarm, I guess."

Kang studied me quietly, lips tightly pressed as if he tried to determine whether I was lying or not. "Why did you shush me? Your magic isn't hearing based."

I shrugged. "I dunno. Maybe for the same reason I

turn down the radio when I'm driving and trying to find an address or the right street to turn down."

He shook his head.

"Like you don't do that."

"I really don't."

"Anyway. You were just about to tell me the inner mechanisms of your brain. Let's go back to that." I stepped forward and frowned.

His gaze filled with quiet laughter. "Did you want me to hold you again as well?"

Yes.

No.

Argh.

I rested my hands on my hips and tilted my head to the side. "Maybe."

Amusement sparked in his gaze. He reached forward, brushed my hands off my hips and replaced them with his own. Heat spread through my body. His fingertips dug in a little and he pulled me forward.

A wave of negativity flowed over me again.

I flung my hand out and placed it on his chest. At the same time, I snapped my head to the side to pinpoint the source.

"Seriously?" Kang let his hands fall to his side.

"There." I pointed at the back of the club. A woman wearing one of those V-shaped shirts that showed off the sides of her boobs, along with a clingy, short skirt, stepped from the washroom. A vibrating ball of hatred loomed over her, but the woman was unaware of the angry spirit nearby.

"It's hovering over that woman," I said.

Kang stepped up beside me and pressed his hand to my lower back. "I see it."

"Is it the same one?"

He shook his head. "I can't smell it this far away. Not with so many people around."

As we watched the woman walk into the throng of people, a man stepped from the women's washroom. He wore a white polo with a lipstick stain on the collar and a shit-eating grin.

"Should we follow both of them?"

"Forget him," Kang said. "The spirit has only been interested in the women so far, and I'm not leaving you here."

"Fine." I grabbed his arm and tugged him along the dance floor. "Come on, twinkle toes. Looks like she's making a strategic exit."

Pushing through the club, I followed the woman. She stopped near a group of people by the bar. They laughed and giggled and then the woman finger-waved at her friends and headed toward the exit.

Before the woman left the club, the spirit zipped away, taking its negativity with it.

I staggered forward.

Kang gripped my arm and prevented me from face-planting. "Did you see the same thing? The spirit left her?"

"Yeah."

Kang pressed his lips together.

"What now?" I asked.

"We follow her anyway. Just in case," Kang said.

I looked up and scanned the crowd.

Kang swore.

The woman had disappeared.

"Come on." Kang pulled me forward.

I slipped out of the club behind Kang, cold air meeting my flushed face. Turning, I scanned the street in both directions. My magic didn't pick up any death energy and the woman was nowhere to be seen.

"Anything?" Kang asked.

I swept the area with my magic. "Nothing. You?"

He shook his head.

"Drat." If that woman was the next crime scene victim, we had the chance to save her and failed.

"Come on." He jerked his head toward a late-night café across the street from the club. "That's the café where one of our lover boys got into a fight outside. Let's check it out. I'll buy you coffee."

Music to my ears.

We walked together to the darkly lit café, one of the few that remained open after six in the evening.

One thing I appreciated about Victoria was the presence of independent businesses. Sure, the big name, corporate companies had infiltrated the downtown core, but they hadn't completely dominated yet.

Some independent clothing stores, restaurants, book-stores, and cafés remained.

Like this one.

Kang reached ahead of me to pull open the door and held it open for me. I thanked him and brushed past to enter the warm café, the air heavy with smells of coffee and baked goods. In other words, I'd entered heaven.

Kang stepped in behind me and let the door close. He slipped his hands on my hips and leaned down to speak, his voice strumming my skin and fluttering my hair. "Your scent is intoxicating."

"Really? Didn't think sweaty would be your thing."

He chuckled, his chest rumbling along my back. "That's not what you smell like."

Before I had a chance to ask what, exactly, I smelled like, the barista stepped up to the counter. Lean, with wiry arm muscles, the man stood around six feet tall and had brown hair that curled around his ears. His white shirt clung to his chest, the unfastened top buttons allowing the garment to show off the top of a chest tattoo.

"What can I get started for the two of you?" he asked.

A room.

I almost blurted the words, but thankfully common sense prevailed, and I bit my tongue.

"Two large lattés, please," Kang said, ordering for us both. Normally, that sort of thing would annoy me, but Kang and Jacobs had bought coffee for me plenty of times when we worked cases together, and vice versa, so we knew what each other liked to drink.

The barista flicked his gaze to me, almost as if to ask silent permission. I nodded and he flashed us a wide smile. "Of course."

Kang paid and we found a small table for two by the window that looked out onto the club-lined street. We didn't speak. Instead, we sat in companionable silence to watch the bustling street while lost in our own thoughts. Kang discreetly looked around the café, probably searching for security cameras. I didn't see any.

The barista came out and dropped off our drinks a few minutes later.

"Thank you." I looked up and smiled.

"You're welcome." He smiled back. "I'm Steve."

Oh, dear. I wasn't looking for an introduction.

Kang didn't say a thing. Instead, he picked up his latté and unsuccessfully hid his smile. His gaze twinkled with amusement.

"I'm Lark." I waved at Kang. "And this is Connor."

Steve's gaze flicked briefly to Kang before settling back on my face. "First date?"

Kang laughed. He actually fucking laughed.

Steve stiffened.

"Something like that." I lifted the coffee cup. "Thank you for the coffee."

Steve nodded, his eyebrows slashing downward in a severe frown before he walked away.

"Can't take you anywhere, Lark. You break hearts everywhere you go."

I snorted and took a drink of my own coffee to hide my reaction. Delicious milky caffeine coated my tongue, and I swallowed a moan. Kang had used my first name again and it made my chest constrict. A funny warmth spread through my body.

"I enjoyed dancing with you." He reached forward and swiped the foam from my upper lip.

An obscene thought to lean forward and snag his finger in my mouth and suck on it flashed through my mind. Then I thought about sucking other things. My whole body jolted with need and heat flushed my face.

Kang stilled, breathing deeply. His gaze settled on me.

"Let me guess. I smell good?"

"You have no idea." He leaned forward, his lips parting to probably say something incredibly indecent that would incinerate my panties. But he stopped. His brows dipped down, and he whipped his head to the side.

I followed his gaze and froze.

Too distracted by Kang and things I'd like to suck, I'd missed the growing sensation of death magic.

A man sat by himself at a table a few feet from us. He bobbed his knee up and down as he stared out the window. Fit and large, he made the table in front of him look like a child's toy. He might be sitting, but if he stood, he'd probably be well over six feet. He wore a white tank top and fitted jeans that showed off his strong legs.

But that wasn't what caught my attention. Curled around his shoulders, the evil spirit settled over the man's skin and pulsated.

Without warning, the man lurched to his feet and bolted from the café.

I exchanged a look with Kang.

Wordlessly, we abandoned our coffees and followed.

TWENTY-FOUR

Kang called Jacobs on his cell phone while we followed the man in Kang's car. The man had taken a cab, so we couldn't use the licence plate to determine his identity or destination, and though we had the cab number, when the taxi dispatch tried to reach the driver, he didn't answer his phone.

Apparently, they no longer used a radio system and the mystery man had somehow found the one taxi driver in all of the Victoria area who wouldn't take a call while driving.

"When we get to wherever we're going, you need to stay in the car," Kang said. He kept his gaze trained on the vehicle ahead of us while he spoke.

"Like hell, I am," I said.

"Morgan."

"Kang."

He grumbled and gripped the steering wheel harder.

"I'm not some damsel in distress who's going to prance around in the middle of a shoot-out. I'm a fucking necromancer. If it's clear my skills are not required, or I'll be in the way, I'll seek cover."

He took in a deep, measured breath.

"Is that better?" I asked.

"Yes."

The vehicle pulled into a suburban neighbourhood and a sense of déjà vu hit me upside the head.

"Do you still sense the spirit?" Kang asked.

I nodded. "It hitched a ride with him."

The cab pulled to the side of the street.

"What are you going to say?" I asked. An image of Kang telling the man to stay still because he had an angry spirit on him rose in my mind. That wouldn't exactly go well.

Kang frowned. "Not much I can say. We don't know what's going to happen. We have no legal grounds to arrest anyone, and if we pull him to the side, he'll either laugh at us or we'll tip the spirit off."

"It's worth a shot."

"I agree. I'll talk to him. If he has a partner, I'll keep them apart while you try to contain the spirit."

"Try is the keyword. Without the bones, the spirit doesn't have to listen to me," I warned.

"Just do your best," he said.

"Deal." I popped open the door and stepped onto

the sidewalk. Kang walked around and joined me. The evil spirit had latched onto the man's shoulders, looking more like a bioluminescent shawl than a source of evil.

The man turned at our approach. "Can I help you?"

"Yes, my name is Detective Kang. I'm with the Victoria Police Department."

Before Kang had a chance to say anything else, the front door to the nearest house slammed open and the woman I spotted having a bathroom rendezvous in the club stepped onto the landing.

Oh no.

Kang and I exchanged a look.

Everything happened at once.

The spirit floated off the man's shoulders. I tried to cast a net to capture it, but the angry spirit tore through my control and slammed into the giant man.

Kang called out, but the man ignored him and ran forward.

"What the hell, Dylan?" The woman stomped down the stairs. "Where have you been? I've been waiting—"

"Don't you fucking dare, Bella," the man snarled.

Bella snapped her mouth shut.

Dylan's face grew red, and he shook. "Don't you fucking lie to me. I saw you. I went to that club, and I saw how much you care about this relationship. You think you're so pretty, so beautiful, that you don't have to be faithful or care about my feelings. You might be pretty, but you're ugly on the inside. I'm going to carve out the rot so everyone can see it."

Before Bella made it any farther, Dylan raised his hand, metal glinting in the streetlights.

"Knife," I yelled.

Kang drew his firearm in one fluid motion and pointed the gun at Dylan. He stepped to the side, probably making sure he had a clear shot.

"Put the knife down, Dylan," Kang yelled out. "Drop the knife. If you step toward me or anyone else, I will shoot."

Dylan sneered, and the angry spirit pulsed inside him. "Why stop me? I'll be doing everyone a favour."

Bella froze at the bottom of the stairs. She stood a few feet away from Dylan, and Kang and I were too far away to intercept without someone getting seriously hurt.

The spirit kept slipping my attempts to grab it and haul it from the body. Without its bones, my power over the spirit was limited. It didn't have to listen to me, and I couldn't force it. "The spirit isn't cooperating."

Kang glanced at me, eyebrows slashed down.

Dylan closed the distance to Bella, ignoring the orders Kang barked out. His handsome face contorted with rage.

"Dylan. Stop! Drop the knife. I will shoot if you move forward. This is your last warning. Bella, you need to start walking backward. Get away from here."

Hearing her name must have snapped Bella out of

her stunned, deer-in-the-headlights state. She shook her head and stumbled backward.

"No," Dylan yelled and launched himself forward, the streetlights glinting off his weapon.

Kang pulled the trigger. A loud gunshot ripped through the quiet neighbourhood and left my ears ringing. The bullet struck Dylan in the shoulder and the man staggered to the side before falling onto the grassy yard beside the sidewalk.

Bella screamed and turned to run.

"Stay down," Kang yelled. "Show me your hands."

While Kang continued to shout orders, I pushed my magic out, searching. The spirit was nowhere to be seen, heard or felt. Where had it gone? How was it hiding from me? As I turned to check on Kang, Dylan leapt up from the pavement, still clutching the dagger and screeched. He ran after Bella, quickly closing the distance with his long, powerful legs.

Kang pulled the trigger again. This time, the bullet hit Dylan in the centre mass. His eyes widened and he toppled over, the knife clattering to the pavement.

I stepped forward, but Kang flung out his arm to hold me back.

No argument here.

I stayed put, my heart rampaging inside my body while my chest squeezed my lungs.

Kang approached Dylan's prone body. The man didn't move.

Sirens wailed in the distance.

Kang kicked the knife away from Dylan before holstering his weapon and kneeling to check for a pulse.

A wave of negativity washed over me again.

"Kang," I shouted out a warning.

The angry spirit pulled free from Dylan's body and shot into the night.

POLICE LIGHTS FLASHED, creating a strobe-like effect on the suburban street. They'd turned the sirens off more than fifteen minutes ago, but the familiar wail still echoed in my head.

I sat on the edge of the sidewalk across from the crime scene as forensic analysts milled around and the police cordoned off the area. Replaying the events over and over again, I kept looking for where we went wrong. Where I went wrong.

I failed to stop the spirit.

The soul hadn't listened to me at all, and a man died because of it.

Maybe if I'd been a better necromancer—a strong, more knowledgeable necromancer—Dylan wouldn't have died tonight.

My stomach twisted and a surge of nausea rose up again. I swallowed it down and took my phone out to respond to Logan's texts to let him know I was okay.

Bella sat on the steps to her house. Someone had draped a blanket over her shoulders, and she rocked back and forth, occasionally shaking her head in response to whatever the officer in front of her said. The officer stood between Bella and the active crime scene, valiantly attempting to shield her view from Dylan's covered body and the dried pool of blood surrounding him, but it didn't work. Bella kept leaning to the side, her gaze cutting to where Dylan lay.

Kang had finally stopped pacing. He stood a few feet away from me with his head bowed. I'd texted Jacobs, but his partner hadn't responded yet.

Pulling myself from the pavement, I walked over to Kang. He shot me a warning look, one filled with hostility, but I ignored it.

"What can I do for you?" I asked.

"Why didn't you stop it?"

I rocked back on my heels. "Excuse me?"

"The spirit was right there. Why didn't you stop it from possessing that man or at least rip it free."

The implication was clear. If I had stopped the spirit, he wouldn't have had to shoot the possessed man.

"I told you I didn't have the bones. Without bones, the spirit can refuse my commands," I explained. "Most spirits listen to me. Most want to help. But this is a powerful and angry spirit. I tried to use my magic, but it just went straight through." I took a deep breath and whispered the last part. "I did my best."

But a part of me whispered back, "*Are you sure?*"

Kang dragged his hand over his face and took a deep breath. "I shot a man tonight. An innocent man who had no control over his actions. The spirit got away and now that man is dead because I pulled the trigger, because I couldn't save him."

"I know you're upset, and you have every right to be. But you saved a life tonight. If we hadn't been here, they'd both be dead."

"And they'd both be alive if you'd done your job."

I snapped my mouth shut. My stomach twisted. Kang might be lashing out because he was hurting inside, but that didn't make it right for him to try to place the blame on me. I already felt like shit. I already blamed myself.

"You're a real piece of work, Kang." I spun on my heel and walked off.

"Morgan," he called out.

I ignored him and kept walking.

TWENTY-FIVE

S weat dripped down my face and pooled in my
sports bra. I gripped the handle and drove the
dagger forward.

Logan slipped to the side and evaded my strike. He
swatted my hand away. "Whoa there, Sparky. I like my
face the way it is."

I spun away and sheathed the dagger. My brother
had been teaching me weaponry for the last six years
and we'd reached a point where we could spar with
real blades and without hesitation, but I was being
reckless. Despite Logan using up the last of the milk
this morning which left me with a fate worse than
death—in other words, drinking black coffee—I didn't
actually want him dead.

"Sorry." I glanced around the room. No one was
watching. No one was ever watching. Logan had
procured a membership to a secluded gym where you

could book rooms and work on whatever you wanted. They had few rules, but one was: If you spill it, you clean it. I doubted they referred to water. The room consisted of three solid walls and one glass one and at one time it must've been a squash or racquetball court. Now, assassins used the old, rundown rooms to hone their skills in private or to teach their sisters how to defend themselves.

Logan chuckled and shook his head. "I knew you had to work off some steam, but maybe this wasn't the right choice."

"And what exactly do you think is the right choice?"

He sheathed his daggers and picked up a towel to wipe his face. "Well, you already told me to eat shit when I suggested calling the detective to discuss what an ass he was and how he made you feel—"

I scowled. "I already—"

Logan held up one hand and used the other to toss the towel back on the chair. "I'm aware you told him before you stalked off, but not everyone can compartmentalize like I can. Not even cops. You might wish to at least hesitate before you burn that bridge down."

I pressed my lips together and folded my arms over my chest. I did not want to talk about my complex and twisted feelings for the detective with my brother. At least, not while we were both still armed—sheathing our weapons didn't negate the danger.

Logan sighed and his shoulders sagged. He knew

when to give up on a subject. "Then if you're not going to pick the detective, at least call back that corporate hottie and work off this anger some other way."

My mouth dropped open. I shouldn't have shared that Hudson had called to ask me out on another date. The shock made me do it. I'd written him off after our last disastrous date. "I'm not sure I like him that much."

"You banged Ricky and I'm pretty sure we all hated him."

"I didn't hate him. I thought I loved him."

Logan pinned me with a flat stare. "You checked out of that relationship months before you actually ended it. You were looking for an excuse to drop that dead weight and don't you dare try to lie to me about that."

"Ugh. Fine." I threw my hands up. "But I'm not sure why you brought up that asshole. The only topic that makes my blood boil more than discussing Kang is my doomed relationship with Ricky."

"I'm merely pointing out, dear sister, that you have never required love or even liked to physically connect with a man if all you're looking for was release."

"What I'd really like is to not talk about sex with my brother."

Logan rolled his eyes and his gaze slipped over my shoulder to focus on something behind me. "If not me, then talk to Brandon or even your work bestie Debbie."

"Denise," I corrected absentmindedly. He knew her name. He intentionally tried to bait me. I didn't really want to talk at all. I wanted to stab things. But Logan did have a point. Stabbing him wouldn't solve my problems, nor would it really make me feel any better.

Maybe I should call Hudson back.

"Is it safe to come in?" Brandon asked. "You two look intense and I never like to barge into the room when either of you is armed."

I turned to find Brandon poking his head in through the entrance. He'd used one hand to prop open the glass door and the other to hold a large brown paper bag. A wave of his cologne preceded him followed by something mouth-watering delicious.

"Are those tacos?" I leaned forward.

"Maybe?" Brandon stepped in and peered around the stark room with peeling paint and various stains decorating the walls. He looked so out of place in his business suit pants and crisp white collared shirt. He must've left the jacket and tie in the car. "You still haven't answered whether it was safe to come in."

"The only way you'll be in danger is if you with-hold those tacos." I stepped forward and held out my hands.

Brandon chuckled and handed over the bag. He glanced at Logan. "Mmmm, sweaty."

"Gross." I clutched the bag to my chest and walked out of the room.

AFTER WE SAT on a park bench and shared the tacos, we made our way home. Though I still held a lot of anger about the shooting and Kang being a dick, some of the tension had faded. This always happened. Spending time with Logan and Brandon made me feel settled and at home regardless of where we were. I loved them both so much and dreaded the day they decided to find their own place together.

We walked into the apartment and the boys brushed past me after taking off their shoes. I was in no hurry and after shutting and locking the door, I sat on the floor and slowly untied my running shoes while I debated calling Hudson.

Maggie strutted up to me and shoved her fluffy face into mine. I gave her a few pets before she grew bored of me and walked away.

Death energy pinged around me and raised the hairs on my arms. I looked up to find the spectre of Bernie hovering above me.

Bernie had been murdered six years ago and her assailant had almost made me join her. While I had been saved, Bernie went to the afterlife.

"Hey, Bernie," I said.

Bernie pulsed blue. Her whole image shook which indicated agitation.

This was new. Normally, she just popped in to see her cat and share ghost gossip.

I scrambled to my feet and peered at Bernie. "Is everything okay?"

"He's seen you," she whispered.

"Who?"

"I don't know his name. He's seen you," she repeated. "You need to be careful."

Before I could question her more, she faded away. Her visits never lasted long, and the time in between grew longer after each appearance. She'd slip away to the veil soon, and I'd miss her. I'd grown accustomed to her random, unexpected visits.

But this was different.

This visit sent a chill down my spine even though I was still overheated from the workout with Logan.

He's seen me?

Who's seen me?

The spirit?

I wasn't married and I wasn't cheating so I wasn't exactly the spirit's prime target. Did Bernie mean someone else? Something else?

"Sparky!" Logan shouted from the living room. "Go have a shower. You stink and we want to start the movie."

I shook away the thoughts of dread and padded to the living room. I flipped up my middle finger and waved it at my brother before making my way to the bathroom. After a long skin-scalding shower that used all the hot water—much like Logan drank the last of the milk—I felt much better and let go of my anger and fears for the time being.

Right now, I planned to focus on having a relaxing movie night with the boys and maybe after that, I'd call Hudson.

TWENTY-SIX

My boots pressed into the dry grass with a crunch. The moon shone overhead, cascading white, ethereal light down on the backyard of the abandoned house. A gentle wind brought smells of barbequed meat and ocean air.

"Not quite what I imagined when you asked me out on a date," I said.

Hudson smiled and passed me the second shovel. He'd worn jeans and a fitted T-shirt, and his white runners shone brightly under the moonlight. He held a shovel in one hand and used the other to run through his hair, pushing it away from his face. He looked like a poster child for a businessman off the clock.

"I thought you'd like to dig something up other than dead bodies," he said.

I winced.

"Sorry. I was trying to be funny."

"It was. You are." It wasn't his fault my thoughts kept drifting back to Kang.

I can't believe I wanted to kiss him.

Heat spread across my face.

I still wanted to kiss him and if I was being completely honest with myself, I'd wanted to do a lot more than just lock lips. To make things more humiliating, he knew exactly how turned on I'd been because of his super senses of unknown glamy origin.

And he'd still treated me like crap.

Unforgivable.

If I could afford it, I'd book a therapy session and try to work through this tumbled mess of emotions, but right now, I was trying Denise's and the boys' advice— distracting myself with a pretty man to get over a jerk and my feelings of guilt for failing to trap a spirit.

What could possibly go wrong?

Hudson frowned but didn't press me on my vague statement. Instead, he pulled on leather gloves and started digging.

I stood to the side with the other shovel in my hand. Did he expect me to dig as well? He told me to dress for a casual night hike, but I wasn't prepared for this. While my jeans and a graphic T-shirt weren't cumbersome and I very well could dig a trench if pressed, I wasn't mentally or emotionally prepared for manual labour on a date. I'd worn pretty panties and a matching bra. This was the third date, after all.

Did the third date rule still apply? Or had hook-up

culture negated that completely? I hadn't been in the dating pool for long since my breakup with Ricky and rarely got past the first date to even worry about this kind of stuff.

Did I even want to show Hudson my matching underwear? The jury was still out on that while my mind and heart remained stuck on another man. Not that Kang deserved the attention.

"What exactly are we digging up?" I shoved thoughts of Kang away.

"You'll see."

It was my turn to frown. I studied the abandoned house. It was one of the Victorian-style houses that reminded me of witch shows on television. This one had been abandoned for quite some time. The windows had been boarded up, but squatters had broken in and street kids had used the siding as their canvas. Colourful spray paint decorated the exterior and broken glass littered the ground surrounding the house. The grass in the backyard was overgrown and riddled with weeds.

Laughter broke out from one of the backyards of a property farther down the street where a number of adults had gathered for a barbeque. Their music, chatter, and laughter grew louder and louder.

"Whose house is this?" I asked.

"My grandparents. My mother grew up here." He breathed heavily and continued digging.

Damn, I was starting to feel guilty for not helping.

"Why did she leave it like this? If she had money, she could've kept it in better shape, or better yet, sold it."

"Not hers to sell or to keep up. This house went to her older brother who was a bit of an idiot. At least that's how she told the story."

His shovel hit something hard, and a smile transformed his face. "Bingo."

He carefully dug around the object until he uncovered most of it. Squatting down, he pulled a decorated box from the ground. Roughly a foot by a foot and a half and around six inches thick, the box couldn't possibly hold a dead body.

Tension released from my shoulders. So he hadn't invited me out tonight to try to get free necromancer services. I'd worried it was that or he wanted me to help dig my own grave. And, like a dumbass, instead of questioning him more diligently, I'd stood to the side, holding a shovel as my one and only weapon, and waited to see what happened.

I never claimed to be the smart one in the family.

Hudson had beat me to the phone call and when he reiterated his invitation for a third date, I would've said yes to anything to get me out of the apartment and away from my thoughts. Now I questioned my impulsiveness.

Hudson set the box down on the grass and knelt beside it. He kept his gloves on but ran his hands down the lid.

"It's a pretty box," I said.

"It's so much more than that." He unlatched the lid and flipped it back. Settled inside, an old book rested on soft fabric.

A book.

He lifted the tome out gently, cradling it in his gloved hands.

"A book? I thought you were after your mom's money." Unless that book contained account information and passwords, it wasn't likely the key to Hudson's mom's fortune.

He tore his gaze away from the book and held it out for me to see. "I'm sorry for the subterfuge. I wasn't sure if you could be trusted at the time." He stood up, holding the book out to me. "Here. Have a look."

I plucked the book from his hands. The cold leather binding pressed into my palms, and I stared at the intricate pattern on the cover. Death energy whispered on the wind. A memory pinged.

The book looked familiar.

Alarm bells rang in my head.

Where had I seen this before?

I held the book closer to my face, trying to take in more details in the limited light from the full moon. My magic curled around me as if anticipating something. Death lingered on the cover.

Bones. The cover had bones embedded in the leather.

Pain sliced my finger. "Ow."

I jumped, the book still in my hands and looked down at my finger. Blood gushed from a cut and splattered over the bone-embedded cover. What the hell? The book hadn't cut me. I snarled and spun toward Hudson.

"Sorry about that." He held a small knife in his hand, the tip of the blade smeared with blood. My blood. The bastard had cut me while I ogled his bone book.

Logan would be so disappointed.

I pulled my magic to me, ready to search for willing spirits to rush to my aid. Before I could call them, Hudson muttered an incantation and my whole world tilted.

TWENTY-SEVEN

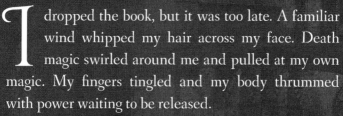

I dropped the book, but it was too late. A familiar wind whipped my hair across my face. Death magic swirled around me and pulled at my own magic. My fingers tingled and my body thrummed with power waiting to be released.

In the veil, I was at my strongest, but also my most vulnerable. Rage surged up within me and pain pinched my fingertips. I looked down to discover I'd sprouted talons for fingernails again.

What the actual fuck?

"It's glorious." Hudson let go of my arm and spun around to face me. "I was never strong enough to get here on my own."

"You idiot!" I stepped forward, formed a fist and punched Hudson in the face.

He reeled back, clutching his check. "What the hell, Lark?"

I pulled my magic and summoned the spirits, they spun around me, whipping my hair around, lifting it from my shoulders in a small tornado. The castle lurked nearby, so close now, I could run and touch one of the skewered skeletons propped up outside its gates. I ignored the castle's looming presence and focused all my anger on Hudson. My talons continued to grow, now at least an inch long, and fought the urge to rake them through Hudson's soft skin.

Weak flesh.

Gut him.

I shook the thoughts away.

"You took us to the veil," I hissed.

The spirits continued to fly around me, waiting, watching. The spirits couldn't hurt me in the physical world without a host body to possess, but that changed in the veil. Here, they could be a weapon to use for or against me. I wound my magic around them, preparing to use them as my lance.

Hudson dropped his hands from his face. "Technically, you did."

"What?"

"You brought us here." He nodded at my bleeding hand, the same one I'd used to punch him.

I should hit him again. He needed another punch to his fucking face.

I stiffened, torn between wanting to hit Hudson again, and running away. "You didn't exactly give me a choice but let me rephrase the question. Why would you want to come here? Do you have any idea of how much danger we're in?"

"The veil holds immense power," he said.

"It also holds imminent death, your death. You will die here. We used my blood and brought the bones with us. We have no anchor to the living realm, and there's nothing here to sustain us. Not if you're human."

"Ah well, you're making a lot of assumptions." He crouched and picked up the book in his gloved hands.

My leg muscles twitched. I wasn't a fighter, at least not in the physical sense. I might train with Logan, but I didn't have the mindset of a fighter, not like my brother. But right now, I really wanted to kick Hudson. I wanted to choose violence. I wanted to tear him to shreds with my talons and watch him bleed.

He'd used me. He'd purposefully set me up to use my blood to take him to the veil. I didn't need to ask whether he actually liked me.

My heart spasmed. I wasn't emotionally invested in Hudson. At least not much. But I'd liked him. I'd wanted to see if there was something more to us and the whole time, the whole fucking time, I was a means to an end. Someone to be used.

"Was she even your mother?" I asked.

Hudson snorted. "Fuck, no."

I gathered more of my magic, unsure of what to do. I couldn't stay here. Nor could I trust that Hudson didn't have any more nefarious plans for me.

I embraced my death magic and searched for my bond with Gregor. I might've said *we* had no anchor to the living realm, but that wasn't entirely true. I had a potential way out and I planned to use it.

Gregor might not be close to where I'd left the mortal plane, but hopefully the bond was strong enough to anchor me.

"What a delight," a new voice spoke amidst the swirl of spirits and churning wind.

I opened my eyes to find another man standing a few feet from us in front of the gates to the creepy castle. He was obscenely tall and powerfully built. He wore leather like a second skin, but instead of coming across like he should be in some kind of kink club, he looked like a warrior. The leather jacket and pants had armoured plates. He also wore a white shirt under the jacket, which seemed so normal and yet completely in contrast with the situation and setting.

I had little time to analyze the guy's wardrobe further. After a cursory glance, I kept my focus on his face. As if carved from stone, he was beautiful in that chiseled, almost too perfect way. He had jet black hair that matched his black eyes, and fair skin that seemed to glow in the constantly dim lighting of the veil.

Hudson clutched the bone book to his chest, and for some reason it reminded me of how a little old lady would clutch her purse or pearls in cartoons.

"It's not every day a thief and a necromancer visit my domain," he said.

I froze. His domain?

I swallowed. No. It couldn't be. There were only three things a necromancer feared in the veil—getting lost, meeting the Lord of the Veil, and coming across barghests. Since that one incident when I was a teen, I'd never had to worry about any of those things.

Until now.

My heart hammered. My lungs constricted. I stopped breathing altogether.

I stood three feet from Leviathan, Lord of the Veil.

No one had ever met him and lived to tell the tale. Until this moment, I hadn't been sure he existed. He was the boogeyman of necromancer bedtime stories. No one knew exactly what he was, or where he came from, only that he ruled the veil and killed anyone who dared to enter.

Was this who Bernie meant? Had the Lord of the Veil spotted me? And so what? He saw me and then decided to chase me with his castle? I was definitely missing something.

I pulled harder on my power, calling for Gregor to answer me and pull me away from this nightmare. Leviathan fed on the souls of the living. We were basically a snack to him.

Come on, Gregor...

"Nice nails." Leviathan dropped his gaze briefly to my hands. "What is your name, necromancer? Your magic in the air tastes familiar."

I shook my head. He couldn't know who I was,

could he? No. Not possible. Not from some pointy fingernails. He had no way of knowing who my grandfathers were, who I was, and I would never reveal that information to him. Mom warned me to keep my lineage secret and I still heard her voice in my head.

Leviathan stepped forward, the ethereal wind teasing the hem of his leather jacket. He smiled as if he knew what I attempted to accomplish with my bond. Could he sense my magic? Could he track my use?

I had to get out of here. If Leviathan got his hands on my blood, he could do terrible things. The veil had an almost limitless supply of death magic and with my blood...

My power pinged. A familiar touch pulled on it.

Gregor.

"We will do great things together," Leviathan said.

I shook my head and gripped onto Gregor's power. Using all my magic, I pulled.

Leviathan narrowed his eyes. He flashed his teeth, revealing long fangs, and stepped forward again to close the distance.

Before he could reach me, Gregor pulled me to the living realm, and I collapsed in a heap by the Master Vampire of Victoria's feet.

He looked down at where I lay and wrinkled his nose. "You smell of death."

"So do you," I muttered into a vaguely familiar laminate flooring before I passed out.

TWENTY-EIGHT

I woke up on a familiar gray couch that smelled like fresh linen and memories.

"Mom?" I croaked.

"Oh good. You decided to join us," Gregor said.

The master vampire's smooth voice in my mother's living room rang all sorts of warning bells. I jerked upward, but my limbs failed me. Caught up in fabric, I rolled off the couch and crashed to the floor in a tangle of my own limbs and the pink fuzzy throw blanket. I got Mom this blanket last year for her birthday, and now it appeared intent on being my cause of death.

"I wish I had caught that on video," Mom said, her voice sounding much stronger than the last time we'd spoken. "Viral gold."

I lifted my head and blinked. Sure enough, Mom sat on an armchair by the gas fireplace, opposite the master vampire. They both held teacups in one hand

and cradled the matching saucers in the other. They personified sophistication, and knowing Mom quite well, this was just wrong.

"Did I travel to a Victorian movie set?" I glanced around the room but found no one else in Mom's small apartment. "Is this a photo shoot for a new media campaign?"

"Your mother was kind enough to offer me tea. My men are waiting outside," Gregor said.

"And what are you doing inside?" I pulled myself from the floor and untangled the soft blanket from my legs. My fingernails hurt, but the talons had receded somehow, leaving my regular nails in their place. Only the crusted blood at the edges of my nail beds hinted that something had happened.

Gregor cocked his head and blinked at me. "Have you forgotten our deal so soon, or did you think so little of me that you didn't think I'd hold up my end of the bargain?"

I whipped my head to look at Mom. Really look. We shared the same colouring—brown-black hair, fair skin, and blue eyes, but Mom's hair had more gray in it than black now and dark bags usually lined the underside of her eyes. Usually.

Right now, Mom glowed. The hollow appearance of her cheeks had disappeared, replaced with smooth fullness. Her face had also lost the pale ghostly colouring, and Mom no longer looked like a shell of her former self. She looked healthier than she had five years ago. But still frail. Still needing to eat and regain strength.

Gregor had cleansed her blood and it had worked.

My eyes stung and a tear escaped. I blinked rapidly. As much as I wanted to sob for joy, I was also very aware of the master vampire a few feet away taking in every detail. Part of me wanted to launch from my current position, throw my arms around Gregor, and thank him profusely, but then I remembered who and what he was. "Thank you."

Gregor shrugged. "It was a part of our deal."

"I thought I'd be present," I said.

"That was not a part of our deal."

I cursed, but I didn't have a valid reason to get angry. He'd travelled to my mom's home and cleansed her blood. She looked a thousand times better than when I'd last seen her.

"How are you feeling?" I asked Mom. Now she, I could hug, and I very much wanted to, just to confirm this healthy glowing version of her was real, but I still held back because we had an audience.

Mom set her teacup on the saucer, and then placed the saucer on the small serving table beside her. Instead of answering, she pulled herself from her chair, walked the three steps to close the distance between us and wrapped her skinny arms around me.

"I love you so much, dear," she whispered into my ear.

I hugged her back and we stood there, embracing

in silence for a couple of breaths while Gregor sipped his tea and watched.

Mom finally pulled away. "I feel great. Gregor said the disease is still inside me, though, so I'll need more treatments."

It would probably always be in her blood. The cleansing wasn't meant to cure her so much as give Mom more time. But it could do what dialysis couldn't and I'd do anything to give Mom more time. If that meant raising more vampires for Gregor, then so be it.

"I thought I was on death's door and you bought me at least five more years to nag you and your brother. Five more good years."

I sniffed. My eyes continued to sting. She looked so good, so healthy. I'd raise an entire fucking legion of vampires if I had to.

"But you shouldn't have done it," Mom said.

I snapped my head back as if Mom had slapped me. "What?"

"Whatever he asked as payment, it's too much. I'm not worth it."

"I disagree."

"I wasn't scared of dying, you know. I was sad to leave you and Logan, of course especially so soon, but I knew, I know, you'll be okay. You'll both be okay. You'll always have each other. I don't want you tied to the vampires. They can't be trusted." Mom winced and looked over her shoulder at Gregor. "No offence."

He smirked and lifted his teacup in a salute. "None

taken, you're quite right. But I feel compelled to mention your daughter has excellent negotiation skills. She hasn't tied herself to me at all."

Yet.

The dramatic pause was telling.

Mom turned back to me with narrowed eyes. "You must promise me, Lark, my beautiful Sparky. Promise me, that when my time comes, truly comes, you'll let me go."

I pressed my lips together.

"No more deals with vampires without my consent."

"Fine," I bit out.

"Oh honey." Mom reached out and gripped my shoulders. "I don't mean to come across as ungrateful. I am very grateful. But I'm your mother. It's my job to worry about you."

Easy for her to say. She hadn't spent the last seven years watching her mom waste away into nothing. Almost nothing.

"I love you," Mom said.

"I love you, too."

"And I love these touching moments," Gregor cut in. "But I'd like to discuss what happened before you got dumped unceremoniously at my feet smelling like a graveyard."

I groaned. Not because I didn't want to share but because of the look Mom gave me. Gregor should've waited until we were alone. I'd have to deal with lectures about personal safety for the next month now.

At least there'd be another month.

I glanced at the door. Maybe I could make a run for it.

"Don't even think about it." Mom waggled her finger in front of my face. "You better start talking young lady."

I sighed and launched into a brief retelling of how I was stupid enough to get tricked into finding an old book for my date and taking him to the veil. I finished with how the trip ended—facing the Lord of the Veil.

"Leviathan?" Mom gasped.

"The Lord of the Veil?" Gregor raised both his eyebrows. Apparently, he could be surprised. Which in itself shocked me. Evidently, it only took getting hauled to the veil and meeting an almost-fictional glamy creature to accomplish it.

"If I didn't have you as an anchor, things could've gone badly." I owed him, but I didn't want to say it out loud. Owing a favour to a vampire was dangerous.

Gregor nodded. "You wouldn't be the first necromancer to get lost to the veil, and presumably lost to Leviathan, but you're not the average necromancer, are you?" His gaze dropped to my hand, undoubtedly taking in the blood-encrusted nail beds where my talons had sprouted and since receded.

But what the hell did he mean? What did he

know? I was powerful, sure, but I wasn't alone in that category.

Mom looked away.

I waited for Gregor to elaborate.

He didn't.

"What was the name of the woman you raised?" Gregor asked.

"Rose Harrison."

Mom paled. Even if I hadn't been looking at her face, her quick, sharp inhale gave her away. She recognized the name.

"Mom?"

"No one knew where she was buried," Mom said. "All this time she was in a nearby grave. All this time she was right here."

"Who was she?" I asked.

"One of the most powerful witches of her time. She would've been hell to raise and control. She was rumoured to have..." Mom gulped.

"Mom?"

"She was rumoured to have the Book of the Dead."

Gregor stilled.

Mom continued. "If she had it, though, it became lost at the time of her death. Many people searched for it, but they all returned empty handed. If they returned at all. A number of necromancers got lost in the veil during their search."

Was that what had happened to Dad? Mom always

claimed she had no idea what happened to him, but what if she did? What if she lied?

But then...

Why would Dad risk the veil to find the Book of the Dead?

My stomach twisted. The Book of the Dead. I'd grown up with stories of the infamous grimoire, the one that held all the forbidden magic. Magic that could give life or take it away. Break chains or create new ones. It reportedly held spells originally used to create vampires and werewolves. In the beginning, people referred to it as the Book of Life, but over the centuries, it had caused so much brutality, so much death, it took on a new name.

And I'd held it in my hands and bled all over it.

Lifting my hands, palms up, I stared at where the book had rested. Mom and Gregor stared, too.

"The book was buried in her childhood house's backyard?" Mom shook her head. "All this time, after so much searching, and it was right under everyone's noses. It must've been protected by shielding spells."

"Where is the book now?" Gregor asked, his tone low and soft, but for the first time since being in his presence, his tone scared me. Every hair on the back of my neck rose and paid attention.

"The last I saw it, Hudson was hugging it to his chest like a lost teddy bear. But I think it's safe to say Leviathan has it now." Hudson was probably dead, and if he wasn't he would be soon. My stomach clenched and nausea churned. I didn't like Hudson. He'd used me. He'd deceived me and he set me up. But death seemed like a harsh punishment.

Then again, if things had gone exactly the way he planned, I'd be dead or stuck in the veil right alongside him. So maybe death wasn't so harsh a punishment after all. Better him than me.

Mom let out a long breath. "Maybe Leviathan having the book isn't such a bad thing."

Gregor whipped his attention to Mom. "How can you say that?"

She shrugged. "The book was originally his, was it not? All those terrible things happened when it landed into the hands of glamies and drabs."

"It could free vampires," Gregor said.

Mom frowned and slowly looked the master vampire up and down. "Do you truly wish to be free of your curse? Would you wish your immortality away? You seem to have taken well to vampirism. If you truly wanted to end things, the option to walk into the sun hasn't been taken from you."

"I wish for us not to be bound by night," Gregor spoke slowly. "I wish to not feel the compulsion to feed, and I wish we didn't have to depend on time or necromancers to raise our loved ones. I wish to be rid of the restrictions placed on us by nature."

"Life has a cost, Gregor." Mom's expression softened. "Immortality shouldn't be exempt from that or the imbalance will collapse everything we know."

Not my mom criticizing a centuries-old vampire...

"Maybe that's not such a bad thing," Gregor said.

"Be careful what you wish for," Mom said. "I don't feel the Book of the Dead will hold the answers you seek. It has only ever delivered death."

Gregor scowled. "Luckily, I'm familiar with death. And now that we know the location of the book, we might not have to rely on your feelings."

"You can't possibly mean to retrieve the book from the veil." I gaped. "That's a suicide mission."

Gregor's expression didn't put me at ease.

"I will not go to the veil for you to steal a book," I said.

Gregor laughed. "You should see your face, Lark. No. I wouldn't risk my personal necromancer on such a dangerous mission."

I breathed out a sigh of relief. My pocket vibrated and I pulled out my phone to find I'd missed three calls and four messages from Kang. His latest message asked me to call him.

I held up my finger to Mom and Gregor and accepted the call. "Morgan, here."

"Finally," Kang said. "I was getting worried."

"Maybe I just didn't want to talk to you," I said.

Kang paused and for a second, I wondered if he'd just hang up. "And you'd be completely entitled to do that. I was out of line and I'm sorry."

I grumbled, not quite ready to let go of my anger. He was more than out of line. He'd hurt my feelings.

Kang cleared his throat. "That's not the only reason I called."

"Oh?"

"We found a possible connection to the murdering spirit cases."

"Congratulations." Okay, now I was being petty, but I was also still very angry. I found out a while ago no one gave out medals or gold stars for being the "bigger person."

Kang sighed dramatically. "A man named Mark MacKinnon discovered his wife had cheated on him and committed a murder-suicide."

"Surely murder suicide isn't that rare. Why this guy?"

"She cheated on him at Spiral."

"When?"

"Three years ago."

"Seems a bit far-fetched." Why would a spirit wait for three years before going on a murdering spree? It didn't make sense.

"I agree, but it's all we've got."

"Okay, well... Good luck, I guess." I played with the chain on my necklace and winced at the callous tone in my own voice.

Kang groaned. "Lark, I'm sorry. I'm an asshole, okay? I was an asshole before and I'm an asshole now."

Lark. He'd called me Lark again and something

softened inside me. My anger dissipated and now I wanted to give him everything he wanted.

Well, that was ridiculous. And so not happening.

I cleared my throat and pushed the warm fuzzy feelings away. "An asshole, huh? Not much incentive to help you out if you're still being a dick."

"I'd just shot someone I'd hoped to save and also placed you in danger," he whispered. "I wished and still wish things had gone differently that night, but those events are not your fault."

"You need therapy."

"Of course, I need therapy. I'm an officer who shot someone while on duty. I'm in therapy now and on administrative leave until I'm cleared for active duty. But I hate how I spoke to you. I hate how I undoubtedly made you feel. I tried to blame you when it was me who felt like a failure. I...I have nothing but confidence in your abilities. I really am sorry."

"Thank you for your apology."

Maybe I was being a tad unreasonable. He had just shot someone, and the guilt obviously ate at him as it had with me, but Kang needed to learn not to take things out on other people.

"We need your help," Kang said. "We know where he's buried. Can you use his bones to banish him?"

I didn't bother pointing out that he shouldn't be working on this case at all while on leave. I understood why he wasn't waiting to be cleared for active duty. He wanted this handled and handled now so no more innocent lives were lost. We would never turn back time and save any of the previous victims, but we could save the future ones.

"Where should I meet you?"

TWENTY-NINE

ark MacKinnon had worked hard his entire life. Raised by a single father who struggled to make ends meet, Mark had started working construction at the early age of sixteen to help with the bills. Determined to provide for his family so his future kids wouldn't know the same struggles he'd faced, Mark was completing a business degree while working three jobs. He'd been on his break during the graveyard shift, enjoying a coffee at a local café when he saw his wife of three years go into the club across the street.

She wasn't alone.

Rage had fuelled Mark and when Candace left the club, he'd followed her home and brutally stabbed her to death. He was attempting to dismember her body for easier disposal when his conscience finally kicked in. Stricken with guilt and grief, he'd staggered away from the crime scene and slit his wrists in the nearby forest, bleeding out before anyone found him. He'd written a detailed confession on his phone.

And now, apparently, if Mark was the angry spirit responsible, he'd returned to the living realm to continue his rage-fuelled campaign against cheating partners by re-enacting events from his own story.

I pulled my gear out of the back of the car before closing the door. Kang waited at the edge of the parking lot near the main entrance to the cemetery. He'd filled me in on Mark's backstory over the phone last night as I made my way home from Mom's place. We hadn't spoken since then.

With a blank expression, Kang cradled a chicken under his arm and held a shovel in his other hand. Jacobs was nowhere in sight, but I hadn't expected his attendance. Kang wouldn't want to drag his partner into this. I couldn't be fired from the VicPD, Jacobs could.

I hesitated by my car. Seeing Kang waiting for me with a shovel felt eerily similar to my last date.

"Do you actually think I'm going to dig?" I asked by way of greeting.

"I can hope." He held out the chicken.

"Where's your partner?" I asked, though I'd already made sweeping assumptions about the topic.

"He's still off."

"I didn't know you guys took breaks?"

He flinched, his expression pinching in.

I plucked the chicken from his grip and held it close to my body before walking past him and into the cemetery. "Is he okay?"

"Yeah, he's fine. Just handling some personal stuff," Kang said. "And I don't want him a part of this. We're not completely on the books."

When Kang called last night, I didn't have the energy or power to confront an angry spirit, so Kang begrudgingly agreed to hold off for twenty-four hours. I'd also hoped that Kang would've found someone else to dig up the remains during the day to save us the hassle.

After leaving Mom's place, I went home and crashed. Nothing woke me up, not even Logan and Brandon's shenanigans or the heavy construction outside. Luckily, when I finally peeled myself away from my pillow and pillow-soft mattress, I found I was energized and ready.

"It's mostly dug up," Kang said. "The staff left it when it got dark."

Spirits were more powerful at night. It had something to do with the barrier between the veil and the living realm being blurred and closer together. We had no evidence the spirit in question was responsible for attacking anyone other than perhaps cheating women and their partners, but we weren't risking it. If this was in fact the murdering spirit, it was unlikely to sit back and let someone unearth its remains and fiddle with its bones.

We made our way through the cemetery toward the plot where Mark's remains rested. As we approached the unearthed grave, someone else's magic rippled through the air, but faint, like an echo.

"Something's not right," I said.

Kang looked over his shoulder. "What is it?"

"I'm not sure. I sense death magic, but it's faded."

"Should we leave?"

"I don't know." Because I was super helpful like that.

"If we don't get him tonight, another couple might be killed." He paused and scanned the area. "We've already sat on this information for twenty-four hours. Let's try."

I nodded and stood to the side while he hopped into the open grave and dug. The nagging presence of someone else's magic lingered, but I couldn't pinpoint the source or why it felt familiar.

Kang stopped digging and frowned.

"What's wrong?"

"I just figured I'd smell the spirit, and I do, but..."

A chill ran over my skin. This had been too easy. "The smell doesn't match the crime scene?"

He shook his head. "A spirit has been here recently, but it's not the same one."

"What does that mean?"

He chucked the shovel out of the grave and stared down at the remaining dirt. "I think the spirit I'm detecting is Mark's, but he's not the one responsible for the murdering spree."

Kang pulled himself from Mark's resting place. He sat on the manicured grass, his legs dangling over the edge of the pit. With his lips pressed together tightly, and his gaze shifting back and forth, he frowned at the dug up grave.

"Should we raise him anyway and see if he knows anything?" I asked.

"Maybe. Let me think."

I sat beside him and waited.

The gentle night breeze rolled over us, along with that uncomfortable feeling of being watched and the lingering tingle of someone else's death magic. This had to be the right place. Right place, but wrong body. But if Mark wasn't responsible, who...

"Fuck." Kang leapt to his feet.

I scrambled to join him.

Kang turned to me, his dark gaze flashing in the moonlight.

We spoke at the same time. "The wife."

Of course. Now it seemed so obvious. "Making other women live her fate?" I wondered out loud.

"Over and over again." Kang pulled out his phone and started madly tapping on the screen.

I peered over at the neighbouring tombstones. "Shocking that they weren't laid to rest beside each other."

Kang snorted and kept tapping, presumably

looking up Candace's information on the cemetery's website. "She's here. In the next section over."

I stood over the open grave of Candace MacKinnon. The temperature had dropped, and a frigid wind moved through the surrounding trees despite the summer month. Death magic rose from the ground and silvery moonlight illuminated Kang as he shovelled out the last of the dirt covering the coffin.

A wave of negativity flooded the area and I whipped around to locate the source. As quickly as it arrived, it disappeared. Ice clamped my spine and I wrapped my arms around the chicken and held it to my chest to stay warm.

Kang tossed the shovel out of the grave and leaned down to open the casket. More sticky death magic flooded the area.

"I think we're in the right place," I whispered.

"Smells match." Kang wiped the sweat from his face with his shirt sleeve before hopping out of the grave.

I peered over the edge. Sure enough, the casket was open and Candace's decomposing remains stared back at me.

"It doesn't make sense why this spirit would act now. She died three years ago."

"Let's find out." Kang's voice behind me sounded tired, almost strained. "Hand me the chicken and you can get in."

I would've preferred the bones brought out, but this would make things easier but Kang had already completed most of the grunt work. I turned and held the chicken out. Kang collected the animal, tucking it under his arm once again.

"That's always your problem, isn't it?" Kang asked.

"What?"

He leaned in. "You never notice anything that's right in front of your fucking face." Without another word, he reached out with his free hand and pushed me into the open grave.

THIRTY

I sprawled backward. Disbelief clouding my mind and scrambling my thoughts. I slammed into the open casket, crushing and cracking bones beneath me. A plume of dust rose and coated my face and lungs.

Kang stood at the edge of the grave and peered down at me, shadows concealing his expression, moonlight playing with the hard angles of his face.

I coughed and waved at the dust cloud. "What the fuck, Kang?"

He didn't reply. Instead, he held the chicken out, snapped its neck and tossed it to the side.

I gasped. Then cursed. "Kang, you idiot. I can't raise the spirit without that."

Kang's mouth twitched into a smile that was most definitely not his.

Oh no.

No. It couldn't be.

A cold prickling sensation ran along my spine.

"I think the spirit's possessed you," I said.

"Am I still pretty?" Kang cocked his head. "Am I still beautiful?"

My mouth dropped open and I gaped at him.

He laughed and picked up the shovel. "A lot of anger in this one. A lot of power."

"Kang," I said, trying to use his name as much as possible to break through to him. "You need to leave. Run. Don't do this."

Not-Kang shook his head. "Why bother? If I can't be happy, nobody can. You certainly shouldn't be. Why should you get to have a life, get to be happy, when I had to die? Did you see what he did to me? Did you see what was left of my body? That should be your fate. You don't deserve life. You don't notice the people around you. Not really. You're in your own little world, aren't you? I can see it all." He tapped his temple. "You see indifference when you should see passion, restraint and..." Not-Kang paused, a deep frown wrinkling his face. "And sacrifices. You really have no idea who he is, do you? What he is? You couldn't even thank him for the flowers."

What sacrifices?

What flowers?

Oh.

Those flowers.

I'd assumed Hudson had sent the roses after I

raised his "mom" and the whole time they'd been from Kang.

Well, what the fuck. He should've put his name on the card.

Despite my irritation at Kang's lack of communication, a warm sensation flooded my chest.

He'd sent me flowers.

And I *liked* Connor Kang.

Then, the reality of my situation crashed back and chased away the warmth, leaving me chilled to the bones. Candace MacKinnon currently possessed the man I liked, and the detective I respected.

"You're not beneath my notice, Connor," I said, still trying to speak to him and not the rage-filled spirit possessing his body. I had no idea what Candace meant about sacrifices, but now was not the time to dwell on it. "You never were below my notice, and you know it. This isn't you talking. This rage you're feeling isn't yours. It's the murdering spirit who's trying to possess you."

"She's very upset," Kang whispered. The real Kang. My Kang. Connor.

"I know. She was brutally murdered by her husband."

Kang shook his head. "It's more than that. She's angry that someone raised her. She wanted peace, and now she has to relive the pain."

I stilled. The lingering magic in the air. The last piece of the puzzle clicked in place. Another necromancer must've been here. Someone intentionally raised Candace and set her loose.

Who would do such a thing...and why?

"Lark." Kang pressed his free hand to his temple and staggered. "I...I don't know if I can keep her out. She's using my anger against me, and she has a lot of power. Lark...you need to run."

I frowned and glanced around the pit. Where the fuck would I run? I stood at the bottom of a grave and Not-Kang killed my only sacrifice.

I pursed my lips. I didn't actually need a sacrifice, now did I? With a quick flick of my wrist, I brought out my knife and sliced my finger open.

"No." Kang leapt into the grave. He knocked me back and wrapped his hands around my neck.

I gasped for air. My lungs burned.

"This guy really is a sucker, isn't he? He wants you so much," Not-Kang growled in a voice that wasn't his. "And he has so much rage. He's already fighting me again. But I don't need that much time to break his world. To ruin it like my world was ruined."

My heart beat wildly as I groped the coffin space beside me with my bleeding hand. My fingers wrapped around a bone.

Jerking my knee up abruptly, I struck Not-Kang between the legs. He groaned and his grip slackened.

The moment I got air in my lungs, I whispered the incantation.

Kang reeled back, clutching his head and screamed. A raw scream that broke my heart to hear.

The bioluminescent shape of a pulsing spirit emerged from Kang's body, extracted by the sheer force of my magic. Candace MacKinnon's soul pulsed and flashed, hovering over Kang's immobile body.

"There you are," I whispered.

Before she could dash away, I grabbed the angry spirit as my blood and magic pulled us across the veil.

CHAPTER
THIRTY-ONE

I stumbled forward, catching myself before I face-planted into the dirt. The spirit wriggled within my powerful hold, but I held tight. Candace wasn't getting free anytime soon. She'd possessed Kang and tried to strangle me. She'd pay for that.

Pain burst at the tips of my fingers again and I didn't need to look down to know the talons had returned. I straightened and froze.

A few feet away, the skeletons on stakes stared back at me. The creepy castle loomed nearby, and Leviathan stood at the end of the walkway in front of the castle gates. He wore a long black leather coat that flapped in the wind, and used his gloved hands to flip up the collar of the jacket to shield against the spirits whipping by him.

Our powers pulsed and collided with one another,

my magic pulling me forward, drawn to Leviathan like a magnet.

The castle area was filled with spirits and they flew around me as well, faster and faster, like sharks in a feeding frenzy, ready to snap at all the magic spilling from me and Leviathan.

Spirits didn't normally do this, but here I was, served on a platter for them.

"I didn't expect you back so soon," Leviathan said. "Did you miss me?" He twirled his finger in the air, playing with the streams of my magic that had already leaked out to dance in the air. "Your magic certainly did."

"I don't even know you," I said.

He raised a dark eyebrow. "But you know *of* me, I'm sure."

"Who hasn't heard of Leviathan, Lord of the Veil? I thought you were a boogeyman used to frighten necromancers into compliance and from using their own blood for sacrifices."

He smiled, revealing his white teeth, including long glistening fangs. "You can call me Levi."

Like hell I'd do that.

"Thank you for the gift you sent me earlier."

"What gift?"

"The thief."

He must be referring to Hudson. Funny how he didn't consider Hudson a necromancer even though

Hudson obviously had some skill and knew enough to bring us here.

"It wasn't intentional." My heart thudded against my breastbone. I needed to tether this naughty soul to the veil and get the hell out of here. "What happened to him?"

"If you hadn't left so quickly, you would've seen for yourself." Leviathan shrugged. "You should've stuck around a little longer. We were just getting to know each other."

"I'm sorry to hear that I missed out. I am once again unable to stay long." I reached out with my power to search for my anchor.

"Then why are you here?"

"This spirit needs to move on." I hoisted the angry soul wrapped in my power. "And by move on, I mean permanently stay in the veil."

"I can take her."

I narrowed my eyes.

"For a price."

"Payment for the gift I gave you?" I asked. Pain struck my chest. I didn't like Hudson. I hated him for using me and betraying me, but using his death as payment for a favour didn't feel good either.

I swallowed and shook my head. Hudson's would've seen me trapped in the veil. I needed to stop feeling guilty for protecting myself and for surviving.

Leviathan shook his head. "By your own admission, the gift wasn't intentional."

It was worth a try.

"My firstborn child is already promised to a coven of moody witches." Total lie, but I wanted to take that particular option off the table.

Leviathan shook his head again. "I merely wish for a favour."

"What is it?"

He shrugged. "I don't know yet. But a favour from one of the most powerful necromancers I've come across in a long time can't be a bad thing to have."

I blinked past the flattery and focused on the wish. "You want me to promise you a favour in the future without knowing what I'm agreeing to?"

"Yes."

"Can you promise this favour will not trap me here, harm or kill my family or loved ones?" I didn't have a lot of options here. I needed this spirit to stop killing people. The necromancer was still out there somewhere and could raise Candace's spirit again—especially if they'd taken one of Candace's bones with them.

If Leviathan took the spirit, he'd neutralize the threat and Candace would no longer pose a danger. This would give us time to find the necromancer and for me to figure out a way to free myself from this favour. I needed to focus on one problem at a time.

Leviathan moved closer and loomed over me. "You, your family and your loved ones will be safe from this deal."

"Okay." I didn't want to think about it. I wanted to go home, wrap myself in ten blankets and forget this night ever happened. "We have a deal."

Leviathan smiled and his potent magic wound around the angry spirit. The moment his magic contained Candace, I let my power fall away.

"I need to go now." I pulled on my bond with Gregor again, but nothing happened.

I tried again.

Silence.

I swallowed. Had Leviathan blocked my access to my anchor somehow? Was that possible? My bond shouldn't have faded so quickly. I'd still felt Gregor's presence in my blood earlier.

I spun around, my heart racing, and considered my options.

Did I even have any?

Leviathan watched, a slow smile spreading across his face. I'd accuse him of tricking me, but he hadn't. My own stupidity got me stuck here.

I curled my hands into fists. Pain shot up my arms as my talons dug into my tender palms. I winced.

"Is there a problem?" Leviathan asked.

"If you're blocking my connection to my anchor, then yes. I'd say there's a problem."

"I merely wished to hold you here long enough to have a conversation. You left so quickly last time."

I forced air to fill my lungs to control my breathing. Slowly, I unfurled my hands. Blood ran down my palms and dripped onto the ground from the puncture wounds my talons had left.

Spirits hummed with delight and spun around me.

A deep howl rose from somewhere in the distance —the sound deeper and rougher than a wolf's.

A barghest.

Dread trickled down my spine. According to necromancer legends, the demon dogs ate souls, and their favourite flavour was necromancer. I had no wish to meet one. Ever.

Leviathan lifted his head, his dark gaze studying the abyss of the veil surrounding us. "It seems our time together has once again been cut short. Let me help you back home as a show of good faith."

I would've preferred he stop blocking my bond with Gregor, personally.

The wind stopped howling and the shadows parted to show the moonlit graveyard. Somehow, I stood in the veil, but looked through the mists at the living realm, like looking through a window into a completely different world.

If Leviathan could open a portal from the veil this easily, why hadn't he done so before?

Or had he?

Did Leviathan walk amongst us in the living realm? Was that why no one ever claimed to see him in the veil?

A wave of ice flowed over my skin.

"You could stay and be my queen," Leviathan said.

I shuddered and walked toward the opening of the veil. I didn't have the energy or brain capacity to examine that comment any further. "Thank you, but not tonight."

The portal snapped shut the moment I stepped through to the living realm. I took a deep breath of summer night air and let the death energy from the cemetery wash over me.

I'd escaped the veil and gotten rid of the angry soul for good, and it only cost me a favour.

It was over.

Well, almost over. There was a necromancer raising murderous spirits who still needed to be hunted down and dealt with, but the current dangers were all neutralized.

I turned around to find the castle and Leviathan gone, replaced with the quiet graveyard and a slack-jawed detective.

Kang stood at the edge of the dug up grave. He must've climbed out after I disappeared. Dirt covered his clothes, and he had a long scratch down his face. I must've done that when I thrashed around trying to defend myself.

With the angry soul of Candace no longer possessing him, Kang didn't appear intent on strangling me anymore. He looked distraught, confused, then... angry.

"Who the fuck was that?" Kang waved his shovel

in the air. "And what the hell did he mean about you becoming his queen?"

I walked over to him, rose on my toes, and kissed him on the cheek. The soft smell of his subtle cologne, dirt and bones wound around me. "Thank you for the flowers."

Kang stopped rambling and stood still with his mouth partially open.

I left him like that—bewildered and struggling to form words—and walked out of the cemetery. I planned to spend the rest of my life napping on the couch.

Too bad I already knew that wouldn't happen, but a girl needed to have some fantasies.

Lark Morgan's
Rules to Necromancy

1. ~~Never use your own blood~~

2. ~~Never meet the Lord of the Veil~~

3. Never run into a barghest

4. Never reveal your lineage

5. Never take more than you need

CHARACTERS

Addison Riley: First victim, first crime scene

Amanda Montgomery: Agatha's ungrateful niece

Agatha Montgomery: Deceased

Bernice "Bernie" Olsen: Maggie's previous owner

Brandon Callahan: Logan's boyfriend

Candace MacKinnon: Mark MacKinnon's wife

Charlotte Montgomery: Agatha's other niece, the smart one

Connor Kang: Detective with the Victoria Police Department

Darren Riley: Second victim, first crime scene. Addison's husband

Denise Ray: Lark's friend, co-worker, and fellow necromancer

Drabs: Collectively refers to all humans without supernatural powers.

Ellis Morgan: Lark's paternal grandfather

Estelle Beaumont: French. Gregor's human servant

Glamies: Collectively refers to all supernatural beings. Glamy (sing.)

Grant Malone: Club owner (Spiral)

Gregor Fissore: Italian. Master Vampire of Victoria

Harold Montgomery: Agatha's husband

Henry Montgomery: Agatha's ungrateful nephew

Hudson Harrison: Client.

Jimmy Stewart: Fourth victim, second crime scene. Tianna's fiancé

John Thompson: Man from club

Leviathan: Lord of the Veil

Logan Morgan: Assassin, Lark's twin brother

Lark Morgan: Necromancer

Maggie: Cat

Mark MacKinnon: Stop looking for spoilers, you naughty reader

Officer Rodriguez: VicPD officer

Oliver Jacobs: Detective with the Victoria Police Department

Peter Schmidt: Court appointed adjudicator for estate disputes

Pierre Deveau: Vampire

Raisers: Larks employer, a necromancer-for-hire company

CHARACTERS

Rose Harrison: Deceased. Hudson's mother

Sir Edington: Agatha's cat

Spiral: Popular club downtown

Steve: Barista

Tianna Jones: Third victim, second crime scene

Acknowledgments

I'd like to thank Nicole, Wendy and Karen for beta reading, Lara Parker for editing, and Book Nook Nuts for proofreading.

A big thank you to Tricia Beninato for the beautiful cover and Kalynne_Art from IG for the character art.

I'd also like to thank my readers for continuing to support me and enjoy the worlds I create.

Candace's ghost story was inspired by a number of sources, including La Patasola and Kuchisake-onna from South American and Japanese folklore respectively, and the true crime case of Zack Bowen and Addie Hall from New Orleans.

I hope you enjoy the story.

Happy reading,
J. C.

J. C. MCKENZIE

Necromancy is a gift that keeps on giving...
...and my powers keep delivering death.

I may have narrowly escaped death during my last case
with the Victoria Police Department, but now it
appears another serial killer has stepped forward to fill
the murderous void. This time, the dead aren't talking.
And while the souls are silent, the vampires won't shut
up. I've given them a taste of my powers and now they
want more.

My relationships with the Lord of the Veil and the
vampires are complicated and my feelings for a certain
grumpy detective even more so. But these are the least
of my concerns. The serial killer isn't stopping any time

soon and after a string of discoveries, the only lead we have is the killer's apparent obsession with me.

With my personal and professional lives set on a collision course, if I don't find a way to sort through the facts and my feelings and learn why I'm the target, I'll end up as the next casualty.

A deliciously dark Urban Fantasy tale with a flawed necromancer trying to survive a harsh supernatural world by International Bestselling Author, J. C. McKenzie.

Purchase *Death Raiser* today!

https://books2read.com/DeathRaiser

About the Author

J. C. McKenzie is a book loving, gumboot-wearing, unapologetic science geek. She predominantly writes urban fantasy and post-apocalyptic dystopian fantasy with strong romantic elements. When she's not spinning tales, she's in the classroom sharing her passion for science and mathematics while secretly warping the young, impressionable minds of our future to carry out her evil plans for world domination. She lives in the Pacific Northwest with her family.

Visit her at jcmckenzie.ca

facebook.com/j.c.mckenzie.author

x.com/JC_McKenzie

instagram.com/j.c.mckenzie

tiktok.com/@jcmckenzie○

bookbub.com/authors/j-c-mckenzie

Manufactured by Amazon.ca
Bolton, ON

45133228R00182